CITIES I'VE NEVER LIVED IN

• • •

CITIES I'VE NEVER LIVED IN

Stories

SARA MAJKA

A Public Space Book | Graywolf Press

Stories from this collection first appeared, in earlier forms, in the following literary journals:
"Reverón's Dolls" in *Jerry*
"Boy with Finch" in the *Gettysburg Review*
"White Heart Bar" in the *Massachusetts Review*
"Saint Andrews Hotel" and "Strangers" in *A Public Space*
"Settlers" and "Four Hills" in *American Short Fiction*
"The Museum Assistant" in *Brick*
"Nashua" in *Virginia Quarterly Review*
"Cities I've Never Lived In" in *Longreads*
"Travelers" in *Catapult*

The quoted lines of poetry in "Settlers" are from three Hayden Carruth poems: "The Cows at Night," "Homecoming," and "Almost April."

This publication is made possible, in part, by the voters of Minnesota through a Minnesota State Arts Board Operating Support grant, thanks to a legislative appropriation from the arts and cultural heritage fund, and through grants from the National Endowment for the Arts and the Wells Fargo Foundation Minnesota. Significant support has also been provided by Target, the McKnight Foundation, the Amazon Literary Partnership, and other generous contributions from foundations, corporations, and individuals. To these organizations and individuals we offer our heartfelt thanks.

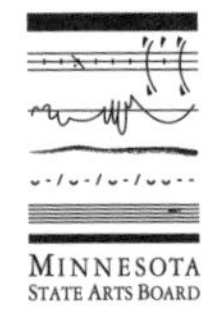

Published by Graywolf Press
250 Third Avenue North, Suite 600
Minneapolis, Minnesota 55401

www.graywolfpress.org

Published in the United States of America

ISBN 978-1-55597-731-3

2 4 6 8 9 7 5 3 1
First Graywolf Printing, 2016

Library of Congress Control Number: 2015953592

Cover design: Carol Hayes

Cover art: Kathy Collins / Photographer's Choice RF / Getty Images for my mom

CONTENTS

• • •

CITIES I'VE NEVER LIVED IN

• • •

REVERÓN'S DOLLS

Maybe ten or eleven years ago, when I was in the middle of a divorce from a man I still loved, I took the train into the city. We were both moving often during this time, as if it were the best solution to a shattered life: to move from place to place, trying to thread together, if not our marriage and our lives, then something in ourselves. Richard was teaching in the Hudson Valley, and I had moved back to Maine, but would go sometimes to see him, and we would take long walks through the estates along the river, and drive up to Hudson, where there was a café that we liked, with an outside patio made of concrete. The croissants were carefully made there, though they served everything on paper plates.

Richard would order while I waited at the table, and when he returned we would eat and often complain about the waste of paper. After a time I would get in my car and find my way back to Maine, though I didn't know the roads well and I'd have to pull over to call him. The wood signs had road numbers neither of us knew, but we would piece it together and tell each other small jokes.

During one of these trips I took the train into the city. I wasn't well in the way that I would be several years later, and the wave of the power lines in the midday sun seemed alive to me. I watched them for the better part of the journey—the way the lines threaded up and down, and passed through sun and shadows. It felt as if there was only me and the distant spectacle keeping pace with me.

The train was dirty, with few people on it. We passed empty lots and warehouses. When we pulled into Grand Central, I entered the station and stood against the wall, so that I could look at the ceiling without being noticed. The exhibit was in the new MoMA, which seemed that day like a church built to disorient. A large white space, with escalators that took you from floor to floor, and every floor looked like the one before it. I was there to see the work of a Venezuelan artist named Armando Reverón. The *Times* had run an article with photographs of his life-sized dolls and of his self-portraits with the dolls. The exhibit took up one gallery, with the paintings in front and the dolls in back. For a time I sat on a bench, then I left the gallery.

In the spring I saw Richard again, him in his lightweight coat, standing in the parking lot near his office at the college. He was dating someone by then, someone who lived in town. He looked at me—a small, unseasonably dressed woman—and what he saw I didn't know; probably he felt sorry for me, but I also imagine it—my discomposure—made him happy, standing there, holding his cup of coffee.

• • •

After the divorce, I went to a cottage along the water that belonged to a friend. Richard and I had gone there several times when we were together, always in odd seasons, during odd weather, when no one else wanted it. I planned to be there all winter, unless someone else came. Richard came one day. There was a cafeteria-style restaurant that served cheap fish meals, where people ate together at long tables, and we met there. He sat down with me and looked at the people at the tables—they were fishermen, and women who cleaned hotel rooms during the season, and men who cooked during the season, and now it was out of season and no one had much to do—and said it hadn't changed much. After, we walked through the town. I felt like a caretaker showing a house that I loved but that had been more neglected than it ought to have been. We could go clamming, I said. He asked after the tide and I said, 3:00 p.m., and he said, That's a good tide. I thought of my body underneath my coat, of what it would feel like to take my coat off in the kitchen while he was there.

Clamming happens in many villages along the East Coast. Clam beds are seeded, in that people aren't looking for wild clams, but are searching for clams that have been put there much as fields are sown. I know little about the lives of clams, though I'm left with the idea that they drift, that the tide raises them and they skirt along until being brought down. You get them by going while the tide is out, and raking with an instrument that looks like a garden tool. You know you've hit a clam by the weight and the ping against the rake. Then you reach down and toss it to the pile. If it's so large the clam will be chewy, or so small it passes through the gauge, you put it in the sand and stomp on the ground. This keeps it from the seagulls that come in, once you leave, like ravens to a kill that's been left behind. When the birds get clams, they fly to a flat roof and drop them to break them open. To the people under the roofs it sounds like solitary hail.

• • •

Later on I was in the city, where I stayed in a married couple's apartment while they traveled. It was a corner apartment filled with light, overlooking a church. The husband was an artist and the walls were covered with his canvases. I'm not sure if the husband had wanted them hung, but the wife had, so I would wake and have coffee with the sun coming in and the brightness of the paintings. There were cats who slept with me, and there were stairs to the roof. If you went up just as it was getting dark, the last of the light receded behind the steeple and made it loom as if in a magical way, and I was full of the feeling of being nowhere, or in someone else's life, or between lives.

The old man who lived below the roof had a window on his landing that was coated in film, and he had placed four dying plants in front of it, leading me to believe the dead plants on the roof were also his. Those were entirely dead, and looked like buried branches, or like a Zen garden of sparseness. It was as if he had first tried a garden on the roof, but when those died he receded further, only daring to try outside his door, and as those were dying he enclosed himself even more, and I never saw him.

When the couple was there, we would smoke on the roof and eat bean salads. I would watch the light around the steeple and feel happy that I was there, feeling for a time that there was nothing but the roof, and them, and their happiness. Then we would creep back down. We weren't supposed to talk on the landing because of the man, though often they'd forget and would tell each other small jokes. It seemed the sort of carelessness that love can evoke, where things can be taken with great seriousness, but also without any at all. But I never forgot about the man and felt him each time I passed his landing, with that dark mat and pile of shoes, and the plants crowding the sill, which rather than suggesting hope, seemed a fleeting and failed attempt at life.

One time when I was visiting, the couple told me that a woman was now living with him. She was much younger, didn't speak good English, and barely went out. They didn't know how he could have gotten her. She was young, not unpretty. On my last visit, though, the wife said, It's just the man again.

It's hard to talk about love. It's as if it closes when we're not experiencing it and becomes impossible to recall. After my divorce, I briefly dated someone much younger. He was about to move to Berlin. I had been there once and remembered trying to make out a subway map at night when a student walked over to help. The student had been tall in the dark, as tall, it seemed, as the post the map was on. It's strange what you remember, what will keep. Whole years can pass, can end up being unimportant, but that stranger in Berlin I remember.

• • •

For years after the divorce, I found I fell in love easily. Sometimes when this happened, I moved to another city, and for a while I was happy because small things were again enough to fill the day. There was the matter of finding a mattress, and trips to the junk shop, with tubs of silverware to sort through, and row after row of shelves, each darker and more closed in, looking for stacks of old plates, putting plates on my lap so I could look at the ones underneath. I liked the grime of the places and what it left on my fingers. The cluster of old men at the door and waiting to see which of the men owned the shop and would ring me up, and the bags tearing so my purchases would have to be taken out and carried.

One store had bins of clothes in back and I would take home jeans with holes and old belts and shoes collapsed in on themselves. At night I boiled eggs and sat in front of the fan drinking gin and tonics, eating the eggs with jarred olives. The grocery store smelled bad and there were often puddles, both in the store and in the street, because of the fire hydrants that were opened in the summer so that children could play and the adults could watch and be hit by mist.

There was a new bar in the neighborhood and a lot of money had been put into the bar, as if for a party that hadn't happened yet. Local artists decorated one wall with metal, and the front window was stained glass. I liked to go during happy hour when the bartenders were just starting. Their outfits—hats and western shirts—looked silly at that hour, and I felt affection for them as they cut limes and poured drinks. I drank greyhounds because the juice was good, and juice was not the sort of thing I bought back then. The bartenders liked each other and spent time together outside of work, not at parties, but in small ways that were nice to hear about. Once or twice I stayed after happy hours, and they grew quiet when more people showed up. Then it had seemed a foreign place like an airport.

The other nice thing was going out to smoke when the sun went down and the sky grew pink. Pigeons perched on a building across the street would lift and fly in circles. Afterward, there were more hours left in the night than there should have been, and it wasn't that beautiful anymore. It was a dark city of trash bags behind gates and partially lit stores that seemed both open and closed. Puddles of dirty water mixed with something sweet you didn't want to step in.

I loved the city back then. It was the sort of love that was uncomfortable, as it didn't return feelings, but only astounding views. The sudden opening of the subway onto a bridge. Looking blankly out the window at the Statue of Liberty at sunset, at sunrise. All the bottles of cleaner at the bodega, each a different color, that I thought were sodas at first. I remember that I was frightened, that I was afraid of getting worse, as I had been getting better for some time. I was afraid that this life I was leading—though everything was beautiful and filled with sensation—might prove too brittle, might fall apart in ways that would surprise me.

• • •

I was thinking of what happens when what makes life possible disappears. The Armando Reverón exhibit had made me think of this. He was mentally ill, probably schizophrenic, and had retreated to an inner life with dolls, making objects for them, and painting himself with them. In the paintings he stares out, isolated, surrounded by inanimate figures.

I had been reminded of Reverón during a movie I saw in the city. I went to the theater alone one rainy afternoon. An ex-boyfriend worked at the theater, but he wasn't there. The movie was a documentary about a man who had been severely beaten and had to have surgery after. He lost much of his memory, and afterward was a different person. He had been an alcoholic before, but afterward didn't drink. He also had a girlfriend before, but not afterward. Afterward he developed infatuations for people. I thought that what the *Times* had said about this man, that to fall in love would be the greatest risk, was true. Mostly the movie was about the worlds he created with dolls and the photographs he took of them. When he had an infatuation, or a close friend, or someone he hated, he would make a doll version of them. They all lived in a town he made, and they went to a bar he created.

When I watched the movie, I thought if he did find someone, if she then left for one reason or another—as sometimes people have good reasons for leaving, even if they, too, are in love—then this man could lose whatever capacity he had for staying alive. That love is more than a risk for some, for some it's impossible, and what do we do in the face of that?

I didn't make it through the movie. I would have missed the early bus, and by the time the next one arrived it would have been dark and still raining. So I left the theater, walking past my ex's coworkers. Perhaps they thought I had gone for him, and, when he wasn't there, had been so overcome that I had to leave. Outside I raised my umbrella. By then I was walking slowly and cautiously to prove that I was collected, or still quickly to show that I was worried over time and buses. I forget which now, though it would have been one of them.

MINIATURES

Back before I was married, I used to go to a store in Portland called the Clown that left out coffee and crescent cookies for customers who never came. It was an old, high-ceilinged place with a gallery in back that showed the work of local art students—robots made from mechanical parts, paintings of gaunt women in kitchens. Everything was covered in dust as neither the art nor the merchandise ever changed. In front were bowls made from pounded spoons and boxes of French soap, and in the basement a wine cellar with rows of bottles mixed in with antiques. I used to wonder if the owners called it the Clown because they had given up on it, knew that despite the color and array it was really without any hope. I went to the Clown, I think, because it felt as if someone loved it despite its futility and I always admired that sort of love.

The only thing I ever found that I wanted, though, was a set of miniature books. I had wandered to the basement one day when I found the tiny volumes. I slipped them in my pocket as I might have done the crescent cookies and went outside. The books reminded me of something I hadn't thought of for years. Once, when I was little, my father brought home an antique dollhouse. He told us he was going to sell it to the miniature museum. We were living on the island at the time, and my father sat on the patio cleaning the dollhouse while my brother, Stewart, and I watched. Another man was there, and this man and my father examined the objects in the dollhouse. In the closet, they found rolls of wallpaper and boxes of lightbulbs. There were books in the bookshelf, perfumes on the dressing table. They opened each vial and sniffed carefully, as if afraid to lose the contents. The man said he knew of someone who would be interested in the dollhouse, someone who would pay more than the miniature museum. My father sat back in his chair. The wind ruffled his hair. He wore a lightweight khaki Windbreaker. His thin hands were red at the knuckles and along the webbing between his fingers.

Well now, he said when the man left, do you think the blackberries are ripe yet?

The blackberries had been talked about all summer until I could see them in my mind: The two of us would walk the path along the cliff while the ocean sparkled below us. All around would be tall grass. We would look back and see the lighthouse, and he would say, There's where we live, near the lighthouse. We would carry baskets with sandwiches wrapped in foil. We would come to a place filled with blackberries, the whole hill covered in them.

When we went it was all four of us. Our parents left me with Stewart while they walked the beach. Stewart barely picked anything and then dropped the bucket I had filled for him. He found a way to fall and land on the berries. He wore a pair of canvas overalls, and berries burst against the fabric.

When the time came to go to the mainland to sell the dollhouse, my mother put me in a pink dress and a blue coat and oxford shoes with sharp laces. She pinched her mouth in whenever she did laces or buttons. She put a bonnet on me that had elastic under the chin.

On the boat, the two of them went inside to get drinks. Stewart and I stayed outside on deck chairs. We could see them through the glass. They looked elegant, as if they were strangers on a transatlantic boat ride. My mother wore a hat, long coat, and scarf. She leaned in toward my father. My father, who was tall and thin and young—they were both young back then—was in his Windbreaker and cotton pants. On the deck, the wind picked up and blew my brother's hair. He was holding a bag of peanuts. He put them in his mouth in fistfuls and some missed and fell on the deck. He was wearing a seersucker suit that had shorts instead of pants, and the seagulls got so close they brushed his legs.

On the mainland, we went to my grandfather's and my parents drove away to sell at antiques shows. They were gone for months. Maybe it was then that my father left—it was hard to know for sure. My grandfather was a gentle, benign presence. Not enough, surely, but when is there ever enough? He would putter around his farmhouse, hammering boards, inspecting the hose for leaks—the place where his neck sagged into his collar looking like a sucked-in paper bag. The shed where he grew African violets, keeping the leaves from burning by taping wax paper over the windows.

Afterward, in the library, he turned the pages of a book

about France. Ah, he said, pointing to a picture of an orangerie, Maybe you'll go there someday. Or maybe there, he said as he turned to another page. I think it was his way of saying what was happening to us—being left there—would only be one event in our life. That life would be many events; this was just one, and going to France to visit an orangerie could be another. He gripped my shoulder as if I were a loaf of bread, tried a different grip, then gave up altogether. Your father, he said, but then he didn't continue.

There were flowers everywhere, an abundance of wildflowers bowing under their own weight—tiger lilies and bellflowers and yellow daisies, black-eyed susans. A peach tree with squirrels eating the fruit. Stewart chasing them, running in circles, flapping his arms.

Look, he said, motioning me over as if he had lost the power to do anything but frantically wave his arms, but also keeping me away, telling me, Don't come. What is it? I said. He held the grass back with a stick. Inside was a burrow with slight, wiggling shapes. They were baby rabbits. They're blind, he said. Stewart and I stood next to each other, staring in. We wanted to get closer, to touch them, but we were solemn, more solemn than we should have been as children. Such things can't be helped. Our solemnity would only deepen as we grew older, so we often didn't understand the people around us, their jokes and interest in the world. We felt disconnected unless we were in the presence of something beautiful, something still, something that called to us. And because of this we often treated people with a delicateness that wasn't appropriate.

Even when my brother grew older and became a drinker, he kept that quality that drew people to him. His gentleness made the world feel softer, more open. He retold stories, boring stories about the bar where he worked, but the point was in the patterns of speech, the way they enveloped us.

I remember Stewart on his smoke break, perched on a stool near the Dumpster. He wore a thick canvas coat with sleeves that slid over his knuckles; his hands would peek out, one holding a cigarette, the other spidered over the pint glass. He drank by lifting his arched hand, sipping from the glass below—the movement so precise it was beautiful to look at.

We lived together in a run-down apartment in Portland. I had accepted a job as a tutor in Barcelona and was leaving at the end of the summer. I packed while the man I was dating watched a De Niro film, stretched out, taking up the sofa. While I was away I rarely wrote. I didn't call. Months passed. I rented a room from a couple who spent nights twined on the sofa watching television. They didn't notice when I walked by. This relaxed me, that they had no bearing on my life. I had no responsibility. There was nothing. Just days spent walking around the city, under those iron balconies that made of the city a layered cake. One day I reached out and touched the man I was tutoring. It didn't surprise him, but it surprised me.

A friend called to say Stewart lost his job and then his apartment. I finally reached my brother at a friend's place near Boston. Did you even get the *Guernica* T-shirt I sent? I asked. He said he couldn't find most of his clothes after he'd gone to the Laundromat. He said, I keep looking for people who are wearing my clothes.

Not long after I moved back to Portland, Stewart visited, coming up from Boston. A cop pulled him over for driving an unregistered, uninsured car and he waited on the side of I-95 until I picked him up. What in the world were you thinking?

I asked. It became difficult to drive because there was water in my eyes, and my nose was running. He said, Just pull over. I said, I'm on the highway. I wiped at my eyes with my palm. He said, Just pull over and I can drive, and I said, No, you can't even do that. And he said, Yes. Yes, you're right.

We sat on the side of the highway like we had sat a half hour earlier watching his car get loaded on the truck. We sat as if we had gotten good at it. How much is this going to cost you? I said. Two thousand. Jesus, Stewart, I said. You could just move back in, that room already smells, you might as well live in it. He said, You know you don't really want that. I tried again later, several days later, but he didn't make eye contact and said things like, That's the way the dice rolls. He boarded the bus, a bag slung over his shoulder, one hand in his pocket. Inside, he crowded the window and gave what I took to be a surf's-up sign. I went back to my apartment, still not used to how quiet it was when I was alone. He sent letters composed of words cut from a newspaper—they looked like the sort of thing that kidnappers sent—but it would be a while before I saw him again.

BOY WITH FINCH

Thirty-Six Free Street in Jonesport, Maine, was a two-story brick building with a view of the harbor. It had an antiques shop downstairs and an apartment above it. When we—my mother, brother, and I—lived in Jonesport during my senior year of high school, a classmate of mine, Eli Cotter, lived in the apartment with his mother and sister. Eli's mother, Gretchen, waitressed at Tall Barney's, the one restaurant in town, and she was often gone with whichever of the local or seasonal men she was sleeping with at the time. There were rarely any adults there, and for that reason, and for others, the apartment was a strange place for me.

The apartment stood at the top of a narrow, musty staircase. A door—usually left unbolted—led into a foyer with a mirror and an end table where they kept the phone, along with dishes of change and stacks of mail. Much of this mail had the names of previous tenants. Whether it was mail left behind when the people moved out or mail that came after, I didn't know. It looked old, though, parchmenty and bowed in the middle.

Gretchen's spider plants clogged the bay window in the living room, and the three bedrooms stood off the hallway one after another, with a cramped bathroom at the end. Eli's sister, Paige, often sulked through that hallway. Two years younger, she had none of Eli's delicacy, his fineness. She was moody and overweight, with her shirt lifting to show fat bulging over the top of her jeans. The sister didn't like me, neither of the women did, though the mother would sometimes sit with me. After my father left, my mother moved us frequently, and we had once lived in Bangor, near a place where Gretchen had friends, and she asked about it. Before that it had been another town in Maine, and she asked about that, too. She slumped on the sofa, her hands gripping her cigarette like bird claws. Once, I mentioned a town I had lived in, then corrected myself because I had listed the towns in the wrong order, then paused to wonder if I had gotten it right. As I floundered, she said, Poor girl, and not sympathetically. I asked her, Why, why poor girl? But she didn't answer.

I thought about it later and decided there must have been several pretty, kind girls Eli had taken to the apartment. They must have babbled to Gretchen and she must have looked forward to them coming, to the ease they brought, to the idea that Eli would be happier. When I came none of this happened. It didn't occur to me until later that Gretchen could have seen some of herself in me. And the way she treated me—with forbearance and mild annoyance—was much the way she treated herself.

Eli had been six and Paige four when they had lived in a commune with their parents. Eli never told me the details, but with their father there had been drinking, other women, violence. I couldn't tell what degree of violence, and I don't know against whom—the kids, or just with Gretchen—if it was occasional, once or twice, or often. She persuaded the husband to leave the commune and try farming, but after a time she left with the kids. I don't know how she picked Maine; all her family lived down south. My guess was that she left for the farthest place she could think of.

She must have thought she had been successful, with Eli there, serious as if he were running a command center from his room. Everywhere the music magazines he was studying, piles of movies by directors he was becoming "completely familiar with." The two of us once rode the bus to Portland for a Bergman retrospective. We were a somber affair, our messenger bags strapped across our backs, our heads bowed in discussion, analyzing camera angles, architecture, a woman's face. The woman's cheekbones jutted out and then the camera had gone to a building with lots of windows. What was the intent, we wondered. How beautiful Eli looked. Once he learned he was beautiful he would become less beautiful. It was the way it surprised you, really, the way it hid, then bloomed. His limp, sandy hair hanging down his cheeks. The unhealthy pallor of his skin, like something not colored in yet. He wore clothes in off shades—a yellow too drained to be called mustard, an infirmary green. Always with him I thought not of color, but of memory of color. Even his eyes were the flattest, stillest blue.

When I had first moved to town, I would often stay after school to play the piano while the music teacher did her grades. One day—before I knew Eli—I watched him pass back and forth in the hall, carrying a manila folder as if he had messages for the president. He was tall, lanky but not skinny, with broad shoulders and a vertical walk, not stiff—he had a nice walk—but there wasn't much sway. My music teacher stood to the side of the door in her argyle skirt and wool sweater, as if she was only going to watch, but when he got close, she said, Eli, let's see what you have.

He came in with the photographs he had developed in the school's darkroom. They showed buildings in Portland, gray sky, not many people, only wispy kids who looked lost in the corners of the pictures. Over the summer he had gone there and stayed on sofas and took pictures of homeless kids. He met them in the bus station and bought them sandwiches.

My teacher lifted each by the corner, then said, Thank you, Eli, for sharing these with us. She poured tea into a Styrofoam cup. She said, Anne plays the piano. I sat scrunched in my chair, a small girl with mousy brown hair, my hands knotted in my lap.

Do you play Beethoven? he asked.

Sometimes, I said.

I like Beethoven a lot, he said, as if it were a singular thing, which for us, up there at the tip of the country, it might have been. He told me they had just gotten a piano in the antiques shop below him. My teacher's face remained still, but she looked as if she wanted to be nodding it.

My mother didn't like the shop; she worried over the prices they charged. The day I went to see the piano, it had been raining and the owner was making spiced apples in a Crock-Pot. Clusters of furniture divided the room. Close to the entrance were ornamental pieces—velvet sofas, Chippendale chairs, French *confituriers,* gilded fireplace screens. Further in were cruder pieces, cupboards with punched-tin doors, benches with peeling paint. Table lamps gave off a low light.

In the back room, the two guys sat at their desks, Eli with camera pieces spread out on newspaper, and the owner, Henry, running reports. Henry looked like a photograph of a country person. Every touch was right, including the denim cap. and crinkles around the eyes. Still, he wasn't shut to the world the way so many of the locals were. And his store had beautiful things, things I otherwise wouldn't have seen in Jonesport. I imagine, he said, showing me the piano, you'll find it pretty decent for these parts. *For these parts,* my mother would have repeated after she took us out of the shop. But really it was a game, you could never tell where someone was from, city or local.

I began to play a piece by Couperin, tentatively at first, only feeling the keys. But as I played, the music expanded. It was as if someone, if they could have seen inside me, would have seen streaks of colors and shapes. Afterward, I went outside and stopped in front of a puddle to find the building reflected there. Light skimmed over it, and it wavered in the wind. It was amazing to me—one couldn't look at a building in a puddle and not know that it existed, that all of life existed there, only a different life. Where did the second life go, if not further? If there were people inside the building when it was reflected, weren't they reflected as well? Eli bending over the table, screwing in a lens, the man passing him the screwdriver, all the lamps on, then off, the office chair still indented where Eli had sat. When someone moved, does something inside the puddle move? No, of course not, but yes, something inside moved.

While I had been playing, Eli had been leaning against the wall, watching me. We didn't say anything then, but after that he sought me out. He must have been looking for someone to tell his secret to, though when he finally told me, he only told part of it. We were following the road that led to Beals. It was early winter and cold. We walked with our hands in our pockets, his nylon coat swishing. He described the floor plan of the apartment, and I didn't pay much attention until his voice changed. The attic, he said, was reached by a ladder in his closet. It had been empty when they moved in, and Gretchen stuffed it with all the knickknacks she couldn't throw away—felting projects, macramé baskets for hanging plants, rainbow stickers with "Jesus" written on them.

He'd go up when his mother and sister were out. That fall, around the time I had moved to town, he found a half-height door hidden behind moving boxes. The door didn't have a knob or latch. He opened it by prying with a butter knife—marks on the wood showed how someone had done this before. He found a crawl space inside, and said that it was empty except for a painting leaning against the wall. He pulled out the painting and brought it to the window. It was old, he said, folk art style, but not country, not kitschy. He tried to talk about the painting—a boy with a bird, he said—but digressed into German expressionism, its influence on film, the use of dark, foreboding buildings, the tropes of monsters.

We passed clusters of mobile homes, taking in the flamingos and lawn chairs, the unlit Christmas lights from the year before wrapped along the metal stair railings, the turf carpets lining the stairs. I let him talk on about monsters. With Eli, I had learned to wait, to learn in bits and string them together later. He said that there was something wrong with the painting. That he'd looked at it until he couldn't hold still anymore, then put it back, scraping his arm against a nail, knocking boxes over, burrowing through until he got to a shoebox of old photographs.

When his mother knocked on the door, the photographs

were all over his bed. She wore her work clothes, and wiped stains from her apron with a facecloth. She used her leg to brace the apron while she scrubbed. She said, There's peas and carrots on the stove, and pizza from last night. Will you make sure to eat something? Then she picked up a picture of the four of them at the commune. In it, she wore a lilac-colored skirt and a loose blouse. Her hair was in a bun, with strands falling around her face. She was holding Paige on her hip. Look at how beautiful you were, she said, look at that.

When she left, he picked up the photograph. It was the one he had been looking for.

When he was ready, he took me up to the attic and balanced the painting on a box below the window. It showed a little boy in green: green pants, a green shirt, a yellow bird on an outstretched finger. It was painted crudely, two-dimensionally; the background looked like it radiated from the boy. He stared straight ahead, and his eyes looked old, much older than they should have looked at that age.

Eli slid his photograph from the folder. In it, he stood separate from his family. He was six years old. He wore green pants and a green jacket. His ears stuck out from his head.

They were nearly the same boy—not exactly, not aligned feature by feature, but almost. I held a finger to the photograph as if I could touch his cheek.

It's possible, he said, while sprawled on his bed afterward, that someone just painted it to look like me. Some freak at the commune.

What about Henry? I said. He'd be able to tell you if it's old or not.

It's nothing anyway, he said, it's shitty folk art. I'd rather have something modern.

He had a smirk, but was more serious than I had seen him, more than about movies or art or the kids he gave sandwiches to. I remember the easy way Eli had sat with them, but also his stiff command. He knew how alive he was, and no one could take that away. He always acted like he was waiting for someone to take it away. Where did this come from? He didn't trust, but then he trusted too fully. In his belief in the sandwiches he bought in wax white bags. In the kids, though he never knew their names.

Instead of going to college, he said, he wanted to travel. I didn't realize what this meant until the spring, when he said he was going to Europe. So far away? I said.

He went first to Berlin, then to Prague. Any news I got was from my mother. Eli's sister left home and died of a heroin overdose. *A sister of a classmate of yours?* my mother wrote in a card before tucking the obituary inside. I was at college and didn't think much about it. I sent Gretchen a card, I hope with more warmth than my mother's, but still short what should have been there.

Then I graduated and moved to Portland, and my mother sent a card saying Gretchen was moving. *I believe you spent some time there?* Around that time I went to New York with a sometimes lover, Franz, a German man who taught music at the University of Southern Maine, to look at an exhibit of old folk portraits of children. I watched Franz purchase apples on the way to the station, noticing how easy he looked, though he was a large man, how easy he looked with a soft-napped bag over one shoulder. Once we were moving, I picked out an apple, but he took it from me and rubbed it in his shirt before giving it back. The mortality rate was so high back then, I said, the train moving through the leaves as if through a perforated tunnel. One out of every two children died. Sometimes the children were painted after they died. They kept the image of them that way; otherwise there wouldn't be any trace left.

After seeing him in the market buying apples, I found that I wanted to tell him how I had cared for this person Eli, who had shown me a painting but had disappeared. About how lonely I had been in Jonesport. Saying it simply so that he would understand. Yes, he said from time to time, I see.

Really, I said, it was difficult for me. It became less difficult the day I saw the painting. I had felt, sometimes, like a bird in between windows, not able to get out, and not understanding why. Yes, Franz said, that's something I can understand. I said, In Eli's painting, the bird stood on the boy's finger. The bird means soul, mortality. If it's on the finger, then the person is alive, but if it lifts . . . it's not really an explicit symbol for mortality, like a red light means stop and a green light means go, but a symbol of fragility, a reminder that at any moment this beautiful thing can fly away. And the beautiful thing isn't the child itself—there wasn't that perception of children back then—and not life either, but something possessed by . . . belonging to God.

After a time he wasn't listening to the words, but watching the way my hands came off my lap and moved through the light.

In the museum, he checked the coats, then found me in a room filled with canvases of children. I sat on a bench near the center. There were windows on one end, with a transparent film over them. He sat on a bench next to mine. The children stared without making eye contact. There was a quality of suppressed noise, as if I felt noise but I couldn't find it. I went to the window. For a while I stared at the rooftops. Then the light brought me into just the light. I felt that these things—the paintings and light—were doors not entirely made.

I'm trying to guess how it went by watching you, Franz said afterward, but I'm finding I can't tell.

Oh, yes. Sorry. I forgot. Yes, these were like Eli's.

He reached into his bag and gave me an apple wrapped in a napkin. The train was coming and he looked as if he wanted to give me something besides apples, but that was all he could think of, so he reached in his bag and took out another one.

Over the phone, I told Gretchen that I wanted to take measurements of her building before she left. I told her it was for my research. She didn't seem to know who I was. I'm so sorry about Paige. I always wanted to tell you that.

Yes, she said, there were so many cards.

She peered through the crack in the door. Oh, she said, it's you. Her hair had grown out and the ends were brittle, curling and lifting from her back. It made her look less in control, but also prettier. Her face was like that, too. Some skin had sunk a little, making her look more exposed. Come in, she said, no sense memorizing the hall.

She led me to the sofa, which was nearly obscured by boxes, then hollered from the kitchen. I only have Folgers, is that okay? I always drink the coffee at the restaurant.

That's fine.

He's doing well, you know. Eli—he's really doing well.

He's working at a gallery, and they have him doing the photography for the promotional stuff.

In the kitchen, she was flipping through a pile of mail. There *was* a postcard, she said, that he sent. The art is so strange, but that's what they're doing these days, he tells me, millions of dollars people spend on that stuff. It's of all these heads projected against a wall. Things I see in my dreams that I don't want to be seeing. Spend a million dollars to see something like that all the time, no way.

I miss him, I said.

Yes, well, he sent a postcard. The refrigerator, you've noticed, is unplugged. I don't know, I got a head start on defrosting it. She pointed to a towel wadded on the floor. And the pickles can't possibly be good anymore, she said, except they're preserved, so they must be okay.

Standing at the bay window, I waited for her to appear below and round the corner toward the restaurant. I lifted the cigarette she had left burning in the ashtray. There was a peach smudge at the tip. I put it back, and then locked the door and took a butter knife from the drawer.

Eli's room was empty. I climbed the ladder in the closet, only to find the attic cleared out, too. I had expected to find it the way it had been, with the macramé, the open boxes.

Inside the crawl space, the painting was gone. I reached around but didn't find it. At the end of the space I saw another door, similar to the one I had just gone through. It also had knife marks. This door opened onto a staircase going down. At the bottom, a door opened inside a cabinet. I climbed through and found myself in the back of the antiques shop.

At first, I thought it was just a secret stairway, and that

everything else was ordinary, but the light was different. It had been overcast when I watched Gretchen leave, but now light diffused through the room, as if the building had been covered in opaque plastic sheets.

I sat at the piano, and played as I had in high school. Then I stopped playing, and wandered through the aisles of furniture. At the end of one I saw a painting: another child done in the same manner, this time a little girl in a white dress. She looked like me as a child. Her hair was like a bird's, chestnut colored, spare at the temples. Everything had been painted still and flat except the eyes. They were brown and filled with worry. I sat on the floor near the painting, feeling close and knowing I wouldn't get any closer.

When Eli finally came back to Portland, I told him what I had found. He asked me which way I'd left the shop. The way I came in, I said. It hadn't occurred to me there was another way to leave.

He shook his head. He had gone a different way—out the front door and up the steps. It was a mistake, he said. He explained that he moved forward in a way that he wasn't meant to.

He asked about the apartment: When I got back in after being in the shop, what did I see there? I mentioned the ashtray where I had put Gretchen's cigarette. He said little things like that were going wrong. The cigarette would still be burning. He said he had tried to thread back, going through the cabinet, up the secret stairs to the attic, and down into his closet. But then he no longer understood which way he should go to undo what he had done. When he realized this, that he was lost in a way he couldn't understand, he threw a book against the wall. Later, the dent was gone.

I could have walked out the front door, but I didn't. I left the painting in the shop and climbed the stairs, went through the attic, down to his room, through the hall, down the stairs, back to the street, threading through the house the only way I knew how. I ended up in the middle of the sidewalk, in front of the shop I'd just been in. Henry stood outside, setting out a chair. He waved me over.

His face looked softer, like worn cotton. When I asked if he remembered the piano, he said, You were hardly Mozart.

You remember.

He sank into the chair. You weren't Mozart, Eli wasn't Ansel Adams. Then he waved his hands. What does it matter, Mozart and Ansel Adams, the way you guys were back then. Better than Mozart. I should have kept the piano. I sold it to a couple in Acadia and I kept, what, probably something pewter. I don't even know what I kept.

Does that answer it? he said. Did you find what you needed to? I would have kept you, too, as it were.

Kind old man, Eli said. Sometimes I think he was put there just for me. And what good did it do?

Eli had been back in Portland a few months. I had seen him working in an open kitchen and drinking at bars with friends, but this time I arrived to find him drinking by himself. We sat at a table near a window covered with a brocade curtain. The window looked over a grassy triangle; the paths were lit with lamps.

When I told him about going into the building, he leaned

back in his chair and traced the top of his glass. He nodded, asked questions, circling the glass the whole time, but his composure began to break when he asked which way I had gone back. Then he sounded like a child asking and aware of that; another part of him sat there watching the vulnerability from a distance. Once, when we were in high school, he had walked in on my mother standing over the dining room table, yelling. My little brother and I sat there, quiet. There was a dish of peas with pearled onions at the center of the table. Butter was melting over the top. One of our tarnished spoons stuck out of it. I reached for the spoon and my mother threw the bowl against the wall. Then she turned to Eli and asked what he was looking at. Most people, when anger is directed at them, will shift in response to the anger, but Eli stayed with me, that same look on his face.

He said, I made so many mistakes. It was as if I was a different person watching myself make mistake after mistake.

We went out to the green across the street, as if the space—the low light, the fog, the shelter of the trees—made us invisible. We walked past a statue of a man on a horse. Eli sat on the top of a bench and got out a cigarette. I leaned against his legs and said, Henry still keeps camera parts for you.

In high school, things changed, he said. I needed money to get somewhere. So I went down and took a few things, small things, and sold them in New York.

No, he said. Many things, *I took many things.* Not from Henry's shop. I never stole from Henry. But the other shop. I kept taking things.

Mostly Henry dealt with reputable vendors, but sometimes he had to deal with other people. Eli went through Henry's records until he found one of these people. He called him, said that his grandmother had died and he had some jewelry. His mother was waitressing that night, and his sister hadn't left her room. He took an empty backpack, went up to the attic then down to the shop. From under a glass display, he lifted hundreds of dollars worth of jewelry.

The man in the city had eyes like marbles. He paid in cash. He inquired politely about Eli's grandmother. Eli tried a second time; when he went down to the shop the case was full again. He took the batch to the city. The man said, The pieces you gave me last time were worth more than I'd thought. I should give you a little extra. They were sitting on opposite sides of a desk. From the drawer, the man took out a stack of bills and slid it to Eli. Do you have more? the man asked. All the jewelry was spread in front of them. Eli didn't understand the precariousness of his position until then. Eli told him he had a painting he would consider selling. Quite old, he said. He described the painting. The man was interested. Eli walked out intending never to talk to him again.

But one night the man called the house, though Eli had never given him the number. Eli recognized his voice at once, the way it layered and withheld. I am inquiring about the painting, the man said. If you decided to sell it.

No, Eli said, my family decided to keep it.

I have to admit I'm disappointed, the man said. I had wanted to see it. It sounded intriguing, and potentially quite valuable. It could be worth more than the jewelry.

There is a family attachment to it, Eli said, almost whispering, trying to keep calm. He could hear his mother in the kitchen, talking to a friend. She had just brought home pizza. He hung up the phone, standing in the dark of the foyer, his hand still on the receiver. She came out of the kitchen, Is that you? What is it? Is everything all right?

He told me that he left for Europe the next week. That he left the painting in the crawl space. That when he returned for his sister's funeral, he found—as I had—that it was gone.

The man, I said.

Eli shook his head. There were those knife marks, he said, even before me. Someone knew about it. It might not have been him at all.

I remembered the vague light through the windows. The emptiness outside. I thought of someone coming in from that. For a moment I believed him; then I noticed he couldn't look at me.

We went back to his apartment. He said, Just say it.

It wasn't yours.

It was a picture of me.

It wasn't yours, I said. I found a painting that looked like me, but I didn't take it.

Well, I regret it, he said. I took it and regret it, if that's what you want.

That's not what I want.

He touched the side of my face, my cheeks rashy from the cold. I tried to move but he held me. You just need to stand here, he said. It's okay, just stand where you are. That's all you need to do. He brought his face in and kissed me, gripping me as if holding me up.

In the bedroom, he didn't turn on the lights—I didn't even see a lamp, just a bed and nightstand—but he kept the door open. He stood over me as I sat on the iron bed. Studying me, trying to figure out how to go about it. I wriggled my jeans off and sat there in my wool sweater and underpants. We lay down. He slid the sweater to my armpits. I was bare underneath, with small breasts and nipples scratched red from the wool.

The hall light caught the cream of my legs and the sweater at my armpits. He leaned over to pick up his drink. Cold drops landed on my stomach. He drew a finger connecting them, then we kissed, kissing so hard that it seemed wrong, the way he still held his drink to his side. He paused to take a sip. Stop that, I said.

Teasing you, he said, holding it out for me. As I drank, he pulled down my underwear. He still wore his jeans, and he climbed on top of me so the fly of his pants rubbed into me. He took the drink from me. I took it back, drained it, and put it on the table.

I could do with a cigarette, he said.

Are you going to take your clothes off?

You could take them off for me.

I could, I said. Or you could just do it. Which would be easier.

That's sexy.

I'm just saying.

I pushed him away. He undressed. First the shirt, shaking his head when it came off to get his hair out of his eyes. Then the pants, down to his boxers. Sitting next to me, pulling them down to put on a condom, then climbing back on top. After so many years of waiting you wouldn't think I would have noticed so much about the ceiling, that there were places where it flaked, and blooms of moisture. I even worried there might be serious water damage, and I almost asked, but his eyes were squished, and there was a lot of focus. A lot of the bed hitting the wall. And all that sighing I did when I lifted my arms to clutch the bars and he clutched my arms. To show my pleasure, I lifted my knees to cradle him, because he was about to come, and I wanted him to be cradled when he did.

After, we sat together, still naked on the bed. My knees tight to me. His arm around me, his lips in my hair. Why the fear? he said.

How much did he give you for it? I asked.

Five thousand dollars.

And you regret it?

I regret it. Anything else?

No, that's all.

After that, we kept meeting at the bar, drinking and going home together. Sometimes we'd stay in the living room, me straddling him on the sofa, his head rolling back and forth. Other times me propped on the kitchen counter with him behind, both of us facing the Frigidaire, the dish towel looped on the handle.

We stayed up late in bed, looking through art books. Wrapping the sheet around me, going into the bathroom to wash up, sleeping next to him in the cold room, waking up too late, the shock of cold from the faucet, running into my classes unprepared, still with the smell of him on me.

One morning, as I was coming out onto the steps—looking down at the old houses of the West End, slipping my arms into my coat—Franz walked by. My hair disheveled, short strands poking up, my face blotchy. He held his violin case, and wore the thick wool coat I always told him made him look Eastern European. The case small in his hands. He stood under a tree; its roots made the sidewalk rise. He walked up to me and, without any harshness, said, You'll have to decide at some point.

We walked through the streets, past the trees with circle fences, the bottoms of our coats flapping open then closed with our steps. I don't mean between the two of us, he said. I'm not an idiot. But here, he said, patting a hand to his chest, with you, you'll have to decide. Do you understand what I'm saying? I think you're making a mistake.

Let me do it then, I said. Let me do what I'm going to do.

The answer wasn't for Franz, but for my mother, many years too late. Once, when I was a child, she took me to a mental health clinic. She knew one of the doctors and wanted me examined. Afterward, the friend let her walk me through a set of doors and down a hallway. The hallway ended at a cube, with windows and children in bright clothing. There were many children, some drawing, some sitting against the wall with dark circles under their eyes. Some crying. My mother behind me, hands on my shoulders, keeping me there, until at last she turned me and we went back.

When we opened the outside door, you could feel the air all hot and open; it's what freedom would always feel like to me. That's what I once told Franz, what freedom always felt like to me: like school being let out for the summer and seeing all the school buses in a row ready to take you home. My mother opened the passenger door and waited for me to buckle before closing it. She got in and buckled her belt but stayed with her hands on the wheel, not putting the key in. We were going to drive without keys. I liked that. She stared at the parking space ahead as if concentration was necessary to avert disaster. She said, This is what happens. Did you see those children? Did you see them in the room? Please, Anne. What good does this do any of us?

While we drove, I waited for the ocean; sometimes we would stop and feed the seagulls from tissue-thin bread bags, the bags tumbling in the breeze, floating and sparkling.

Eli eventually moved away. After a few years, I learned from a friend that he had married a painter, a Swiss woman, and was living in Cambridge. I found a picture of him online, taken at a gallery opening, and I almost didn't recognize him, he looked so happy, so much at peace.

WHITE HEART BAR

Years ago, I came across an article with the headline "Local History Professor Caught Stealing Maps." Under the headline, I was surprised to find the name of a man who had once been a friend of mine. Years ago, not long after the girl had gone missing, I had watched him leave the library. I was under the shade of a tree, and he didn't see me. There was an intensity about him—as if everything was wrapped into one emotion, not sadness, or despair; the closest I could come was confusion, but it wasn't really that.

After a time his face relaxed, and he continued down the stairs. I felt sympathy for him and thought I understood that moment on the stairs, what it was for him, but I'd been wrong.

In those days, during the time of the lost girl, I was living with my husband in a grand but decrepit loft apartment in an area of Portland that was known as resurgent, a description that carried more than a little wistfulness. Near us, an upscale restaurant was tucked into an old brick warehouse. We would sometimes sit at the bar, eating complimentary cheese straws and ordering the cheapest bottles of wine before sweeping back up the street in our mismatched secondhand clothes, my crimson coat and rubber boots, Richard's gray cashmere coat that must have once belonged to a wealthy man but now very much belonged to him—the military lapels, the satin lining, the soft matted pills under the arms.

We lived on the third floor of a building that looked vacant from the street. Even when climbing the central stairs—a rattling, metal affair that echoed with every step—we felt an air of abandonment. Our apartment, too, was cavernous. In the middle of the space, we had created a sitting area out of Chinese screens. It was silly, really, looking like something the Red Cross might have set up as a triage area if Chinese screens had been considered appropriate. Inside sat two chairs, a newspaper rack, and a coffee table piled with books and newspapers.

It was here that I first read about a twenty-four-year-old girl who had gone missing near the harbor. With the newspaper on my lap, I told Richard. He asked what day she had gone missing. When I told him, he said that she was a student of his at the night class he taught at the arts school. He had driven her that night after class, to a bar by the waterfront; he'd seen her walking along the road and offered her a ride. The police had been there after class on Thursday. What could I tell them? he asked me. What do I know about this girl?

Over the following weeks, he told me the story several times. He also told me that on two occasions they had gone to a bar together, and she had told him stories about her life. He told me a little about it. I also read newspaper articles, a blog that her friends started, the police transcript. I talked to people at the local paper where I worked—enough so that I began to piece together what had happened.

The night she disappeared had been warm for February, and the warmth had brought the fog in. It would have been hard to see her at the side of the road on the outskirts of the city, where there were a few boarded-up buildings, some empty warehouses. She would have been walking along a strip of sidewalk, the streetlights illuminating the fog.

There would have been a darting quality to her, with her high shoulders and lanky arms. She walked without gloves, without a hat, her hands stuffed into her coat pockets, her breath a cloud in front of her. The fog, the buildings, the streetlights. Her fragility and toughness, the physicality of her walk. I could get that far. And to my husband backing out of the parking space, leaning forward to clear the windshield, arranging the books and papers at his side, fiddling with the radio. He saw a movement in and out of the streetlight. He almost didn't see her. He cleared more of the window, craned his neck, then eased the car out of the lot. He pulled to the side of the road just ahead of her and leaned across to open the door.

He said, Louise, Louise, and she grabbed the door and put her head in. Her hair fell across her face. Her face, even when she held her hair aside, would have been in shadow, the overhead light having broken months ago.

Do you want a ride? he said.

She lingered with one hand on the door. Okay, yes, she said, thank you. She lowered herself, a puff of air coming up through the cracks of seat leather. She settled her purse on her lap, didn't buckle her seat belt. She was close enough so he could see her then. Her curls escaping from a loose bun. Her eyes with shadows underneath.

I had imagined at first that he was a sudden flurry of activity, leaning over to swipe at the empty coffee cups as she sat down, but as he told the story, I understood this wasn't the case. He was comfortable with her, he knew how to talk to her. He said simply, continuing a conversation they'd had at the bar weeks earlier, Why New Mexico?

It was seven years ago, she said. She had left home. Her roommate worked at a snack bar in a bowling alley, and they shared a room in a ranch house with windows only in back; there weren't any windows in front. The room contained boxes that didn't belong to them. Someone had tacked sheets over the walls.

She slouched in the seat while talking to him, as if the ride was going to take hours rather than minutes. She laughed quietly, looked over at my husband, thought of the bowling alley, the nacho chips with cheese from a pump, the orange T-shirts the counter help wore. Anyway, she said, I was seventeen and I liked to bowl.

Are you any good? my husband asked, but it wasn't a real question; he was busy looking for the White Heart, a bar by the waterfront. He slowed the car. The bar was down a cobblestone alley blocked off to traffic. He pulled over next to the barrier and looked at her. He had parked in an interval between streetlights and she opened the door to turn on the overhead light. It's broken, he told her. You could put in a new bulb, she said. I could, he said.

She slipped out, pulling her purse after her. She said, Thanks, see you next week, and bounded toward the side of the bar. He watched her silhouette, her hand reaching up, feeling the lump of her hair as if tucking it in then swinging open the door—a clumsily balletic move, the dropping of the hand and swinging it out again. Then the door settled closed. He sat there for some time. He told me this offhandedly, had said, There's something else. Maybe ten minutes after the girl had gone in, I—

Ten minutes, I said.

Yes, he said, I stayed for a while in the car.

What did you do?

I don't know, he said.

We were silent, then he said, While I was there, a man walked past.

The man walked down the alley and entered the bar the same way as the girl. My husband thought it was Alec. But there had been the fog, the darkness, he couldn't be sure.

It didn't seem like his sort of place, my husband said. But it looked just like him.

You didn't see his face? I asked.

No, but I'm nearly certain it was him.

I realized that I had seen the girl before. She had been at a party at Alec's house. He lived across the harbor, in a half-weatherproofed cottage. The porch was covered in vines that gave it an enclosed, hidden feel. Alec and the girl had sat together on a wicker sofa. She had her legs pulled close to her. Her shirt was baggy, too big for her, and the hem of her skirt was unraveling.

Alec rarely looked at people when he talked, and his body was turned away from her, his face down. From where I sat, I couldn't see his eyes, though I knew they were hazel—in certain lights they were specked with yellow and usually rimmed in red; he rarely slept well.

I glanced at them a few times from the kitchen window, but I paid more attention when the girl left—a funny girl with sandals in one hand, shells around her ankle, walking down the dirt road. When he came in, we stood in the kitchen, which was very white, and leaned against the cabinets, finishing gin and tonics. I waited for him to say something, and he didn't. He finished his drink, and I took his glass and poured him another. He sat on the counter, his feet against the faucet.

I had met him shortly after his wife left him, though I didn't know that at the time. I never found out if she left for another man or in response to his remoteness. Perhaps she thought she would be able to live with it because she loved him, but after several years realized that she couldn't. I had seen a picture of her. She had large eyes, a warm smile, and warm brown hair around her face. I imagined, based on the picture, the kindness in her and the sadness she would have felt in leaving him.

His office was at the end of a corridor. Sometimes I brought lunch, and we would sit there with only his desk between us. In this way I learned bits of his life, that he had spent his childhood in Maine but his family had moved to Chicago when he was a teenager, that he had moved early in his career from job to job, that there was some sort of dissatisfaction there, a sense that despite his love of history, the profession itself suited him as little as anything else.

Do you know what my mother once said? he said. Don't talk too much. If you stay quiet, people will assume complexity. She also said I was a cold fish.

He looked up, surprised and unsure about what he had just said. I kept my gaze even and mouthed the words *cold fish*. What are people thinking sometimes? I said. I felt compassion for this man who never thought he would speak those words out loud. Life can be so unkind, I said to him. And he nodded, though who knew with Alec whether it was in agreement or simply a reflex.

I called Alec after my husband told me he might have seen him that night. We agreed to meet at a café. Alec sat with his chair pulled out and his body turned as if toward a third person.

She was at the bar, he said. She had told me she might be going out. I hadn't seen her for a while so I went.

There was a band at the bar and he didn't like the noise. He wanted to leave, but she was with friends. He could smell her shampoo, that was how close they stood, but when bar seats freed up he found himself next to a woman he didn't know. Louise sat turned away from him. He had thought to go to the bathroom just to get away, but walked out the back door to the harbor. Then the group gathered around him on the pier as if it had been planned, some of them smoking. She was drunker than before and stood apart, looking at the ocean.

He approached her. When he had walked into the bar, she looked up and smiled. Now she turned toward the wind, took an elastic from her wrist, tried to pull her hair up, and then let it fall. He lifted a hand as if to smooth her hair, but pulled his hand back.

I'm going, if you want a ride home, he said.

She mentioned another bar they were going to; he hadn't paid attention and told her to take a taxi home. Probably she didn't hear. The group had splintered. She started to stumble. Maybe the shots had taken a while to hit, or maybe how subdued she was had hidden how drunk, or maybe his presence had organized her. Her arm floated up to point at the moon. *The moon,* she said, *there is the moon.* Then she felt like sitting. She climbed a ladder down to the sand, took off her shoes, and balled the socks into the shoes. She sat on a rock with her purse in her lap.

She remembered living on an island years ago and lying on the dock, the stars overhead and jellyfish in the water, the rowboats tied with rope that dragged with seaweed. She had lain down with some of the other people from the farm, and thought, The world opens immeasurably. She would have felt it like something opening inside of her. Then she had slipped into the water while the other people from the farm talked on the dock. The little dipper, someone said, count the stars. The water was so cold that she gasped. Louise? someone had said. She was in between the rowboats, in the space where one was missing and the others swayed to meet but didn't. She kicked out. Cold? someone asked. *So cold,* she said, kicking away. She hadn't even been wrong that the world opens immeasurably—it does—but it also does something to you, all those jolts and shocks.

She kept a flask in her purse and decided to drink, but then her friends from the bar called from above, so she put down the flask and put her shoes on. Later she would remember the flask, climb back down to look for it. Somehow her shoes would end up there. My sense of it starts to break down here. She was feeling chaotic, things were happening too quickly, in the bar then not in the bar, climbing down the ladder, taking off her shoes, drinking the rum. Then she was up again, on the pier. Where are your shoes? someone asked. She didn't know any-one, but she stood in the crowd as if she did. People asked about her shoes. The last person who'd asked was the one they interviewed. He was with a group of college guys; they were young and intensely interested in her shoes, they kept asking her, but then the interest dissolved, something else, as if they were goldfish turning in a pool, attracted their interest.

And you were lovers, I said to Alec.

It was over, really, at that point.

Have you been to see the police?

Yes, he said. Right away, the next day.

They showed him security footage from the pier. The police had charted each person who went down, when each passed, and when each came back. They had pointed him out. He looked upset, they told him. Angry, like something was going on, they said, pointing their fingers at the screen. He told them that he loved her. He knew he'd made a mistake, so he quickly tried to fill the hole. He told them that she was troubled. I wanted to help, he said, but there was nothing I could do. He talked too fast, keeping his eyes on his hands. At first they found him guilty, strange, but at some point the tension in the room eased. They stopped paying attention, thought about din-ner, home. No one thought, Poor guy. No one thought much of anything. Mostly they didn't like him, though they would never have been able to say precisely why.

I said, You know there was nothing that you could have done, but he didn't say anything. A few weeks later he cut his first map. He slid it in his bag, walked out of the library, and stopped on the steps. The pain on his face would be clear. He wouldn't notice a woman standing under a tree, watching him, trying to understand.

At home we listened to the radio. They had found the body. My husband called from inside the screens: Anne, he said, Anne, come here. I sat with him; he relaxed and lifted one of the newspapers from the floor. Gases bring the body up, he said, gases and temperature. I don't really understand. Tides play a part. They're saying it was an accident.

The lamp lit the orange of the screens and illuminated the space.

Later, I found him sitting on the bed with his head bowed. He was crying. I'm very sorry, he said. There was a tattered cover on the bed with dull squares of burgundy, rust, and light blue. He put one hand over his eyes and I sat behind him and placed a hand flat on his back and stayed like that for some time, while rice cooked in our alcove kitchen. I felt a sudden enlarging of space, with sacks of half-put-away groceries on the counter, the sagging bag of rice scattering kernels everywhere, everything acquiring significance, more beautiful than the many beautiful things I had seen, more beautiful even than the harbor had ever seemed to me. One hand shaking as I scooped rice into an open palm, husband still sitting on the bed, the apartment darkened and the lamp still on inside the screens, now glowing as if there was a heart inside. Husband in near dark, sitting on a faded quilt. His coat still on, as if he had known, in preparation for a shock, that he might need it.

SAINT ANDREWS HOTEL

In 1963, an eleven-year-old boy named Peter Harville was committed to a state mental hospital in the western part of Maine, far from the island where he grew up. He had cut his wrists with his father's coping saw, and lay on the ground watching the sawdust turn red until someone opened the door. Peter? his father asked, not moving or coming in. Peter? Are you all right? Peter noticed that his father spoke more gently than usual, and the shed felt warm and calm; for the moment he was happy.

The next week his mother packed a bag for him and his father took him on the ferry, then into the Cutlass sedan that was kept in the lot on the mainland with a key under the seat for anyone on the island who had an errand to run. They were at the hospital by three. Afterward, the father checked into a hotel. He went to the bar across the street and had several pints of beer. It had been ten years since he'd spent a night off island

and he studied the line of coasters taped to the wall behind the bar. His hands twitched on the counter. They were small-boned and fine, adept at gutting fish and killing the lambs during the summer slaughter, thinking of their bodies dangling in the walk-in no more than he thought of anything else.

In the hotel room, he took off all his clothes and folded back the sheets, then slid inside and tried to sleep. When he got home, his wife listed object after object, asking if they'd let Peter keep it.

Sometimes I dream about him, she said to her friend Eleanor. They were hanging laundry; the wind came up the grassy slope and blew all the soft clothes on the line, the chambray shirts and white cotton sheets, her blue nightgown with lace along the neckline.

While her friend clipped, Helen stared across the sea. She felt as though she had lost something but she kept forgetting what it was, and when she remembered she couldn't understand it. Do you suppose it's a long trip? Helen asked, her voice sounding like it arose from a daydream. The idea had come to her over days, like a bubble expanding in the back of her mind, that it had been a mistake, that she would take the ferry, find the car, drive to the hospital, tell the doctors it had been an accident with the saw, that it wasn't true what her husband said about Peter.

Her hand slipped, and a gust of wind took the sheet and blew it down the hill. Both women laughed and chased after it, barefoot in cotton skirts, two thirty-year-old women chasing after a sheet, then drinking instant coffee in the kitchen with a plate of crackers between them. They gossiped about the hotel where Eleanor worked as a housekeeper. She was seeing one of the men there, someone's cousin who was going back to Boston soon. Helen watched her, watched the liquidness of new love—the way her talk spilled, her eyes shone, how her hands slid through the air—and thought, He's going to leave and she'll still be here.

One day the ferry went out to sea but the mainland never came. The captain turned back fearing he would run out of gas. He tried again the next day, but still couldn't find the shore. In time, he took it as a matter of course, as they all did, as they forgot their desires with some relief, as the desires when they arose had been impractical, painful. One man who painted in the loft of an old barn began to paint canvases of blue trees. The islanders hung them in their living rooms, and there was something hopeful in it, as if they had kept a belief in the symbolic power of beauty.

Peter stayed in the hospital until he was twenty-one; nobody could find his parents, and the hospital had put him to use in the kitchen. When he left, he couldn't find the island on any maps. He took a boat out, but in the place where the island should have been was a sprinkle of land, most of it not much more than rocks. The most promising landmass turned out to be nothing but sandy slopes and beach grass. He was told someone had tried to start a leper colony on it years ago, but it had proved inhospitable. He traveled the coast for some time, taking on construction jobs or working the docks, looking for anything familiar.

He finally took the bus up north and got off in Portland, Maine. He stood there, a medium-sized boy with pale coloring. Across the street he saw an old brick building with "Saint Andrews Hotel" lettered in faded white paint.

He took a room for a month. When the month was up he paid again. He liked it there; he liked to sit idly with the other residents. In the hospital, they had sat for hours on the long, narrow sunporch, everyone squished in with African violets and end tables, all the old men leaning on canes, their eyes in the light as opaque as glass marbles. No sooner had Peter left the hospital than he found another one. How strange we are. How different we are from how we think we are. We fall out of love only to fall in love with a duplicate of what we've left, never understanding that we love what we love and that it doesn't change.

He took a job at a fish stall in the Portland Public Market and would come back with his white T-shirt stained watery red and orange where he leaned against the counter. What have you been up to, Petey? Betty would call out. She worked behind the desk, and always had shadows of mascara under her eyes, even during the morning shift.

He would shower, then return to the lobby, the low tide smell still clinging to him. The residents talked lazily back and forth. A man drinking from a coffee-stained paper cup turned to him and said, I used to have a wife from Chicago. Know what she did?

No, Peter said.

Fell in love with the butcher, the man said.

Another man said, Don't pay him any mind.

Things went much as they had in the hospital, until one day a girl came in. She was beautiful—fourteen, fifteen, slender, knock-kneed. She used to live on the island, used to ride up and down the dirt road on her bicycle. She wore a lavender skirt instead of cutoffs and her face had lost some of the boyishness, but otherwise she hadn't changed.

No, man, someone said when Peter started to walk over. That one'll put you in jail.

No, he said. I know her. He froze before he got to the desk. He realized what was wrong: she should have been nearly thirty.

In the morning, he followed her from the hotel. She walked to the old port section of town, along cobblestone streets and down to the ferry terminal. She walked through the building and out into the fenced-in area where people waited. She put down her bag and stood there, a cardigan folded over her arm. They must be mistaken, he thought, standing like that in front of a boat that never left the harbor. It must have once been a nice boat, with a cream-colored canopy and dark wood accents, but the hull was leaking rust; a dozen wooden park benches had been dragged under the canopy. He thought there was no sense in it, but then an old, silver-haired man emerged from the cabin and took the girl's ticket. She boarded.

When Peter tried to board, the captain shook his head, then tied the rope, pulled in the metal ramp, and disappeared the way he had come.

The next time someone from the island came, it was a friend of Peter's father's, an old fisherman, a drunk with a bulbous nose and gaping pores. Peter had always liked him, found something gentle in him that had been missing in his own father. As with the girl, the man hadn't changed. Peter followed him down the hall to the bar in the corner of the old ballroom, and sat next to him. The bartender poured Peter the bottoms from old bottles of wine. The man was impressed—Helps to know people, the man said. They talked for a while. The man said he had never lived on an island, that he drove trucks for a shipping company. Always wanted a boat, though, he said. He opened his wallet and showed a slip of paper tucked inside the silky creases. He wasn't a man for impulses, but he had bought a ticket to look at whales for the next day.

In the morning, Peter walked with him to the same ship the girl had left on. After the man boarded, Peter extended a wad of bills toward the captain, who looked at it kindly as if he wanted to understand.

For months no one came, then a small, strong, dark-haired woman appeared. She wore a cheap-looking polyester skirt and a scallop-sleeved peach blouse. It was his mother. Like the others, she hadn't aged. She edged around the lobby like she used to do when they went shopping on the mainland, dropping her shoulders so her body moved inward. She used to pick through shirts and speak as if annoyed with him, then hold the shirts up to his frame and purse her lips.

She stopped at the desk, then went down the hallway, following the man who carried her bag.

He tried to get her name or room number from Betty. She's too old for you, she said.

She reminds me of my mom, he said.

She shook her head. Sorry, she said, it's regulations. She took a dollar from the drawer so he could buy coffees from across the street.

In the morning, his mother reappeared in clothes even more drab—a gray skirt and an ill-fitting blouse and sandals so tight that her feet squished out between the straps. She went over to the utility cart to pick out her breakfast. She hovered over the metal tray with pastries piled on doilies—the doilies reused until grease blots seeped through the paper—at last selecting a danish with a circle of yellowed cream at the center. She ate her breakfast in a high-backed chair along the wall, eating slowly as if she were on a trip away from home for the first time, getting to pick what she wanted, and enjoying the secrecy of her choice.

Peter handed her a newspaper.

What's this? she asked, holding it away from her.

I thought you'd like it, he said.

Thank you, but I don't read the paper.

After his mother left the lobby, Betty bought the paper from him. She did the crossword puzzle, frowning at the paper as if it had done something to her. Do I remind you of your mom? she asked.

Not in the least, he said.

She invited him to her room after her shift for a cocktail. When he arrived, she had showered and washed off her makeup. She had spread nips on the table, and he lifted up the fanciest bottle. Go ahead, put them in your pockets, she said. He picked a Jack Daniel's and some gin. She motioned for him to take more. She talked to him about something—applying to college, or a trade program. He opened a bottle and drank. She ran a hand over her face as if looking for something. You should listen, she said. You can't stay here forever. I'd like it if you could, but you can't.

He thought of opening another, but instead tapped his pockets, moved to the door, and said, You coming to clams?

Sure, she said. I'm coming.

When he walked out to the hall, his mother was walking past. Are you finding everything to your liking? he asked, falling into step with her.

Everything is fine, she said.

There are brochures in the lobby with some attractions, he said. If there is anything I can do for you.

I'm quite all right.

He said, I was wondering where you're from. She kept moving; he reached and touched her arm but she shrank from him. You remind me of someone I know is all, he said, someone I once knew. And I don't mean to bother you. I just wanted to make sure you were having a nice time.

She stopped—they were in the lobby—and studied him. I'm from Stamford, Connecticut, she said.

Do you have a son?

A daughter.

Does she look like you?

A little, she said.

Do you have a picture?

That's enough.

She meant it to come out more lightly than it did. She asked him to show her the brochures, and she took several, even ones she had no interest in. He gave her directions to cafés and shops. He invited her to clams.

The residents of the hotel ate clams at a run-down place by the docks that had five-cent littlenecks on Tuesdays. They sat inside on tables covered with plastic gingham cloths. The back door was open, but the wind didn't come through. The door looked onto a parking lot filled with lobster traps and rope crusted with dried-out crustaceans. Beyond that lay the harbor. From there, Helen appeared. Peter stood, and the others stopped talking. She looked up, saw the table of scraggly people and the young man, his hair a fine sandy gold and his body shimmering with sweat. She hadn't noticed before how different he was from the others. It occurred to her that she could take him with her, as if he could fit into her purse. She thought of her house in the development, the driveway with squares of concrete that reflected the moon.

You came, he said.

Yes, the directions were good. She sat down, keeping her purse on her lap.

No one is going to take it, he said.

She laughed. It's just habit.

We ordered already. We would have waited, but we didn't—

No, it's fine—I'm glad you didn't. Sometimes I can never find the places I need to find. She glanced at the table for a menu, but didn't see one. She lifted an arm to flag the waitress, but he pulled her arm down. Clams, he said.

Clams?

You order clams.

What else?

Clams, Portuguese roll, ear of corn, iced tea with sugar. Just say—never mind. He looked up. The waitress had come over. She'll have the clams, he said, and the waitress nodded and walked away. I'll have the clams, Helen repeated. Very good choice, someone said.

When the food came they stopped talking. Chipped stoneware bowls were filled with shells the colors of seagulls, with clams so small they must have been illegal. They picked out the graying bellies with little forks, and dredged them through butter, their lips shining with the oil. The thin, waxy napkins that came in the packs of plastic silverware only blotted the oil.

On the walk home—No, not home, Helen caught herself—she said to Peter, I'm glad I came.

You thought you wouldn't be? he said, holding his arm out to see the shadow.

Yes, she said. I thought it might be strange.

But you're glad?

I'm glad.

At the hotel bar, they had several drinks, things she wanted that he wouldn't normally have ordered. Things mixed with cranberry juice, grapefruit, grenadine. Oh! she said, aren't you going to eat your cherry? The cherry was at the bottom, speared to an orange by a pirate's knife. He had never gotten a pirate's knife before. Two cherries! she said. She's happy, he thought. I'm happy was the next thought, followed by the unfamiliar recognition of joy, the discomfort in it, the panic. Will it leave me? How to make it not leave me? Thinking that if he pretended it wasn't there, it wouldn't leave.

At the end of the bar, he saw the captain of the ferry, hunched over, one arm circling a beer. He turned to his mother. She was lining up swords. He asked her how long she was staying at the hotel. She said she wasn't sure. She was taking a boat the next day to Peaks Island, she said. It was a tourist island close to the mainland. The picture on the brochure had captivated her.

Can I come with you?

It might be better if I go alone, she said. I've had such little time. It sent pain through him. She saw it. She said, I don't know you.

Do you feel like you know me? That you might have known me before?

I read paperbacks, she said. I go to restaurants and sit by the window and read.

That's what I like to do, too.

In the morning, she stood in the lobby, holding a straw hat. He walked toward her. He could see Betty approaching him, so he walked faster. When Betty realized what he was doing, she stopped in the center of the room, under the place where a chandelier used to hang.

Outside, he lifted his mother's bag.

I hope the person I remind you of was kind, she said.

She was always kind.

Well, there's that at least.

When they got to the ferry building, the window where she had bought the ticket was boarded up, or she couldn't remember where it was, or something else happened to confound them. She looked at Peter and said she would stay if he wanted that, but he handed over her bag and said to go on, that he would be there when she got back.

SETTLERS

An artist I knew used to tell me stories about his life. We'd sit on the curb and he'd talk in the low, measured voice of his. His wife had left him and his daughter, Leigh, in a fishing village hours north of Portland. They had moved there so he could be a painter and he had a studio that opened to the harbor. Soon as his wife left, though, it didn't mean anything, the studio, trying to be a painter.

She had left him in October. Winter was coming. They didn't have any money.

His daughter had outgrown her winter clothes, and at the church store, he bought her an oversized jacket with a great fur hood that made them both laugh, but he couldn't find her any boots. After, they ate at the soup kitchen in the church hall. They ate there often. Almost everyone in town ate there. There wasn't anything to it. They were all poor, that many hours north, where the sun was so slant and spare that by January you felt it could disappear. No one talked to him about his wife leaving. The men especially acted as if they weren't there. Paul had to remind himself they thought they were doing him a favor. At last one of the men looked up and said, They were giving out bags of rolls before, but looks like they're all gone.

That's fine, Paul said. We have bread.

That night, Leigh watched cartoons, a blanket over her. Paul studied the stained glass fruit that hung from the window. He wanted to take them down, but didn't want her seeing any changes. Outside, the sky seemed to rest on the boats, their masts as bare as the trees. Gradually the sun sunk and the light widened and turned red and orange. It felt impossible then, living this way, but soon there was the coziness of the house at night. He set up TV trays, and she stayed bundled under the blanket, the cartoons flickering over her. She watched the screen even after he turned it off.

When they finished dinner she rested her face on the blanket and talked to him, nestling into the sofa as if she was an animal. This is kind of nice, don't you think? he said. I don't know, she said, though he could tell she was happy; it was only that she begrudged him everything. Her withholding had always been a form of tenderness toward him.

He said she'd have to go over to someone's house some days so he could paint, and he asked whose house, naming the two women who did day care, Sheila and Maryanne, and she said Sheila, which he already knew.

He turned up the heat. When it warmed, he combed her hair and got her in a nightgown. Then they lay on the floor, the two of them around her lamp, and he read from something she'd picked from the bookmobile. He also had a stack of poetry books he'd taken from a free box, the pages blooming with water damage. He read Brodsky poems, then Hayden Carruth, finding a poem about a cow. You'll like this, he said. *The moon was like a full cup tonight.* You like Sheila don't you?

Yes, she said.

If you decide you don't like it we can talk about the options, but let's try this.

He woke on the sofa to her rustling in the kitchen. He sat up to see what she was doing, and watched her put a bowl on the floor and pour cereal over it.

After breakfast they walked the dirt road past the jumble of cottages, trailers, shacks, to Sheila's sturdy ranch with a front room painted yellow. Sheila let Leigh in, then smoked with him on the steps. He asked her how much she'd charge, and she said an amount that he knew was too low. I'll cook dinner for you, he said, you can come over and have dinner with us. Leigh cooks.

I would believe it, too, Sheila said. She asked if his wife was coming back, and he said he didn't think so. I only ask, she said, because I wanted to know what Leigh thinks, what you told her.

She hasn't asked, he said.

It might be better if you don't wait for her to ask, she said.

He went to see an apartment above a bar—one that was cheaper and better insulated than theirs—but it was dark and filled with trash. He picked up cans, then gave up and headed toward the harbor. Some of the houses had new woodpiles, the wood so fresh the color was iridescent. He walked to the bird sanctuary, then couldn't think of another place to walk. He got to Sheila's hours early.

We were about to have a snack, Leigh said as they walked down the path.

We can have a snack at the restaurant, he said.

The sign by the register said to wait, but you only had to look to be sure the waitress saw, then you found a table. They sat in a booth with vinyl so stiff it barely pressed in. Leigh ordered a brownie. Paul drank coffee and watched out the window. You know why we need to move, right? he said. That we could get a warmer place to live? That the winter gets really cold? He wondered if at that age you understood winter, if you could remember it from the year before. She detailed the project she was making, a construction-paper basket for trick-or-treating. What color? he asked. The other kids were using orange but she was using green. Why? he asked. She wanted to.

That night they had dinner on the sofa again. He couldn't handle the intimacy of being alone with her, so he let her watch cartoons while they ate. After, she said she wanted to sleep in the living room, and there wasn't much of a point he could make against it, so they brought in her mattress.

They got a bag of potatoes from a neighbor's cousin. They had done this when he was a child, stored a bag in the cellar and eaten them all winter, but the cottage didn't have a cellar. Shit, he said, then went outside so he wouldn't swear in front of Leigh.

The sun set. Light stretched over the harbor. Red lines formed under the clouds. He thought how everything could be the same each day, and how the only change was the light and the kinds of colors it made. On nights like this, drinking used to help, or he would drive to Portland to visit friends, leaving Leigh and her mother together like polite strangers.

Now Leigh was in the living room, her eyes like saucers watching the screen, waiting for him to return so the steps of the evening could be gone through.

I don't want mashed potatoes, she said when he came in. What she wanted was the french fries they used to make in the oven. He switched off the television. Wash your hands, he said.

They're washed.

Let me smell them, he said. They smelled like skin, like the oils that came from skin. Wash them, he said. He grabbed towels from the kitchen chairs and threw them on the sofa. He made her eat at the table. He didn't speak while they ate. She found small things to complain about. The crusts that in better moods he cut off. You're getting spoiled, he said. She watched him. He said, I'm just saying that it's not something you should be expecting, having someone cut your crusts like you're the queen of Sheba.

What's that? she said.

I don't know, he said, but you're becoming like that, just like the queen of Sheba.

I'm not like that.

Eat your potatoes then, he said.

They're yellow.

That's the margarine.

What's margarine?

They were ludicrous, the two of them sitting there.

He took out the sweatshirt they had bought at the church; the neck was tight and didn't go around her head. He ripped it open. There, he said, putting it on her.

That night he read to her. *A road that had wound us 20,000 miles stops, with a kind of suddenness, at home. At home and in midsummer. The snow has gone.* He read under her lamp. They had brought it from her bedroom. He had asked if she wanted it and she had said yes. Her eyes sank at the sound of his voice. There it was, better. She had eaten some of the potatoes and had hated him. He put the book down, turned the lamp off. He cleaned the table, put the dishes in the sink. He did everything quietly. It wasn't going to work, he knew. After ten minutes there was nothing to do but what he did the other nights, read in a chair while drinking. She was asleep, had rolled to face the wall. The heater came on in a sigh. He turned off all the lights except the one over the stove, then went out the door. He looked in the window to be sure, but she didn't move.

Sheila kept him outside while she stayed behind the door. I was just walking by, he said. And I saw your lights.

Where's Leigh?

She's asleep.

Is she alone?

What else can I do? I can't sit there every night.

He tried to get her to come to dinner the next night. She told him that she wanted him to be able to come in and for her to come to dinner, but that it would be lonelier after, and this—how she was now—was as lonely as she could handle. She looked older than usual, and this made her prettier to him.

When he got back Leigh woke up and asked where he had been.

I had to ask Sheila something, he said.

What did you ask her?

Go to sleep, he said.

Are you going out again?

I only had to ask Sheila something.

Where did you go?

I'm not going again, he said.

She lay back down. Several times while he read he looked over expecting her upright but she stayed down. It was so dark outside. Sometimes you can't imagine it, how beautiful it had been there.

At the end of November they had to drive to Portland. He needed to pick up the work that hadn't sold at the gallery. They hadn't asked him to bring new work, so he imagined that was that. In the truck he let Leigh pick any station she wanted, and she kept turning the dial. Okay, he said, there we go. He took over the dial and stopped on a news station. He looked to see if she was pleased or not, and she seemed pleased.

They parked near the harbor and walked through the cobblestone streets. She rose on her toes to balance, and he teased her, because suddenly she looked like an orphan, when she hadn't looked that way up north.

What did you even pack? he said. Did you pack a dress?

No, she said.

What did you pack?

Jeans.

You pack like I pack. But there's a difference. Do you know what the difference is?

No, she said.

You're a five-year-old girl, he said.

How old are you?

I'm thirty-three.

She stopped paying attention. She followed a leaf fluttering down.

He tried a thrift store, but a pretty girl behind the counter told him they only sold adult clothes. He watched her hands as she motioned outside, toward other stores he could drive to.

For lunch they ate Belgian fries in newspaper cones. Leigh studied them, not sure if she was being tricked or not.

You dip them in mayonnaise, he said.

Why?

That's what they do in other countries. In Canada they eat them with melted cheese.

The sunlight hit the people at the counter, making them look like they were in a tunnel. Everyone still had their coats on. The light would go down soon. After eating they went out into the light. Leigh closed her eyes. The wind blew her hair; she tugged at it with her fingers. The pads of her fingers glistened. His fingers also glistened and he pressed them into the palm of his hand because they felt slightly damp.

Back at the hotel he read to her. *I have seen snowflakes all winter like blurred stars in the air* . . . He sat at the edge of the bed until she fell asleep. Then he slid to the floor and tried to read. The heater turned off. It was too quiet. He got the keys from the dresser and went out. He'd seen a bar down the street with a Schlitz sign in the window.

The next morning they picked up his work then found a pair of boys' boots for her in a thrift store on the way home. As they drove, the highway emptied and the sky widened. Pines on both sides grew taller and thicker. When Leigh fell asleep, he opened the bottle of whiskey, drank. What did it matter? It was straight road for hundreds of miles. He stopped outside Bangor at a discount food store. Near Orono there was a place that sold expired beer. He looked at a pumpkin beer clouded with sediment. The man working there tipped the bottle in the light, said, Should be fine.

They drove 9 toward 193. He had wanted to name her after a small town there called Aurora. The center of town was a gas station with a café, and the town hall, and then two-family apartments with porches. He thought it could be a place to start over. There would be as good as anywhere. He wondered what it would be like, to pull to the side of the road, and enter the café to ask about a place to stay, and the next morning finding a job and building a life without anyone knowing who they were. He didn't want to bring her back home. He wanted to start again, but it also frightened him, because there would be nothing to keep them from trying again and again, until it became a repetition, each time the surface of them growing dimmer, more transparent, a father and daughter in the entrance of a café. He told her they would be like settlers, like in Oregon with the wagons, and waited for her to ask what that was, but she just looked out the window during the time it took for the town to pass.

• • •

When he was married and would take work to the gallery, he used to sleep in the cab of his truck. He preferred it to sleeping at a friend's place, arriving and standing in the middle of the living room, tall and slim, alien to his surroundings. If they asked, he'd say he was sleeping at a friend's that they didn't know. Stepping out of his cab in the morning to the sun low and bright down the tree-lined streets, he'd blink and pound one fist into the other. Then he'd walk to get coffee and rolls at the bakery, walking until he was either warm or at the water. At the water he'd throw bits of bread for the birds. And then often it was to the library or the museum. If it was warm enough to sit in the park, he'd find a shaded place to drink and write descriptions of what he saw. He liked to be a little drunk when calling his wife.

It was harder for him to tell what came next. He had decided they would have to move to Portland so that he could find work. He left Leigh with Sheila so that he could go to Portland to look for a place. Walking in the West End, Paul saw a sign in a window and called. He thought they would be renting the rooms that had the sign, and he imagined the tall windows looking onto the street; that they would have a piano, and if the ceilings weren't tin, they at least would have molding. Instead the woman took him to rooms behind the building. There were collapsed lawn chairs and a plastic pool someone had tried to grow a garden in. Tall trees lined the back. The woman had trouble with the keys. At last she got the door open and drew back a curtain.

You can plant outside if you want, she said.

Does it get sun?

It does, she said, it's just too late now. She said it held heat well and he couldn't imagine much of anything getting out anywhere. She said that someone was coming to look at it at three. He remembered his years of living alone in these kinds of apartments and told the woman he would take it.

When he told Sheila that he needed to return to Portland to look for work, Sheila didn't question him, so he didn't have to explain. He had put the new key on the ring, but he didn't tell her this. They smoked on the stoop while the children played.

He wondered what he would grow in the summer, if the window would get enough light to be able to grow seedlings. Leigh would grow marigolds, he thought. There was a school at the end of the street and Leigh would start there next year.

He told me he never decided what he would do. The first few days, it was nice being alone in the apartment. The landlady, Lena, had been right about the morning sun. It hit the frost that accumulated on the window and made it glow. He brought in a table from the street. One morning he took his clothes to the trash out back. He trimmed his beard, littering the sink with bits of his hair. He wet a towel and rubbed his armpits and arms and chest, put on a new shirt, brushed down his jeans.

He walked around. Didn't do much, really. A month passed easily.

One afternoon Lena knocked at the door. He knew it was her. No one else knew there was a door in back. Where the other residents of the building thought he was always coming and going to he didn't know.

A woman had come and asked if he lived there. I told her no, Lena said, that I didn't recognize your name, but she left her name anyways.

He looked at the torn paper Lena laid on the table, then went back to the stove. They didn't say more about it.

He didn't call Sheila. Instead he went to the harbor and found a job washing dishes in a restaurant. Four days a week for the dinner shift. At five he ate with the kitchen staff. He wasn't sure how he spent the rest of his time or how time had passed so quickly. He grew his beard again; he gave up the flattery of slim-fitting shirts. When he had trouble painting, he got glasses. He looked in the mirror and saw he had been changed by what had happened. After it rained, he'd walk out in bare feet, feeling the thawing ground underneath him. He took to novels, still liking the ones he found in boxes, slender books with dried pages. He bought food at the co-op in the center of town, small bags of cashews, bags of dried fruit and fig bars, and would eat them downtown, sitting on benches or curbs.

At work they told him a woman had come in and asked for him. He understood then that he was simply waiting. When Sheila found him working in his garden, he went inside for drinks. They sat in camping chairs near a tree where the moss was so soft she slid off her shoes. She took out a half-smoked cigarette she then had trouble lighting.

They went to a show downtown. She wore one of his cardigans. They sat in the back corner, against a record bin, both of them pulling their legs close. Her breath smelled like the alcohol they were sharing, and what she had eaten, and also a little of flowers, though it might have been her hair. Do you like the show? he asked between sets.

This is what you do? she said. This, and your garden?

And I wash dishes, he said, most nights. I just have tonight off.

You left a lot to be able to do this, she said.

I try not to think of it that way, he said.

How do you try to think of it?

I couldn't really say, he said.

She walked home with her hands in the pockets of his sweater in a way that he liked. He thought about kissing her, thought that her breasts would be small. In the apartment he turned on the lamp, took out his bedroll. She stood in the kitchen. You've been here the whole time? she said.

Except the few nights I slept in my truck, he said, but then I found this, and she let me stay even before the first of the month.

Is that the woman I met that one time?

Yes. Lena.

He asked her if she needed anything else, anything to sleep in, but she said she was fine. He went to the bed he had made in the kitchen.

In the morning she was up before him, sitting in the garden with a book from the nightstand. She read out loud from one of the poems. When she finished he said, I don't have to tell you what it was like for me, what it's been like, do I?

She said, I had to find your wife. I had to tell her that you had left, and she came and took your daughter while I stood there.

There's nothing I can say, he said. I've tried to think of something all this time.

Later in the day, a man started to work on the foundation where the house was sagging. When Paul looked out the window, he could see Sheila talking to the man. He wondered what they were talking about, and he remembered that about her. They had once gone to the grocery store together, and she had started talking to the woman looking at the produce, and with the fish guy and the checkout bagger, ordinary conversations about the weather, or what the catch was like, or which fruit was in season.

She came inside. I'm going for a walk, she said.

He said, I'll probably read and then go to work. Do you think you'll be back before?

She wasn't sure, and walked around for some time. She went to the thrift store and tried on skirts and boots. She went to the deli and sat there. When she walked back the sun had lowered and no longer hit the garden; the man had stopped working on the foundation. She thought of the line of mailboxes and the woman who told her that she didn't know Paul. Well, we should all find some way to be protected, she thought. We should all find ways to protect ourselves. She unlocked the door with the key Paul had hidden. He had left the lamp on, with a note that there was food in the fridge. She found a plate with chicken. She put it on low, then took her clothes off to shower.

It was a slow movement they made over those weeks, Sheila sitting with her skirt sliding up her legs, Paul drawing while she smoked. If she stayed for a long time she would go through volumes of poetry and not remember the authors' names but would remember the sense of spaciousness it gave her. It reminded me of a time before I met my husband, when I lived in San Francisco, in an apartment with rooms full of people I barely knew. We used the kitchen to arrange food, cut bread if we had any, putting the knife in a sink overflowing with dishes and going down the hall where the rooms branched off.

The light in my room came in strong and spare. I had tried to grow herbs on the sill. The wood floor was as dusty as the hallway but faded by sunlight. I slept on a mattress on the floor and there were boxes and piles of things everywhere, including beautiful clothes that belonged to a friend who was traveling. Some of the books and records were hers, too, though others I had found that summer, going through used-book stores and thrift stores. I read with my head on the mattress and took breaks to smoke out the window, full of what I had read. What had I read back then, what had made me feel that way? I had a volume of Rilke and Saint Augustine and early Hemingway stories. I must have left them in the room when I moved away.

THE MUSEUM ASSISTANT

For a time, I worked at a small museum on the Upper East Side. It was a museum most people had never heard of, located at a college most people had never heard of. The museum was in a low concrete building. You could easily miss the entrance when walking by. There was a rail, a door, and the name in silver letters. Inside, the windows were above your head. The doors opened to a foyer, where I sat behind the desk and gave out stickers and offered to put people's coats in the closet behind me. In the galleries were mummies, pottery, and miscellaneous art. At noon my boss took over while I ate in the park across the street. I watered the plant in the corner and ran weekly admission reports, but mostly I sat there, feeling vacant, and it was during one of these shifts that a man came in who reminded me of my father.

He was older but attractive, and he appeared successful, though it's unlikely that my father would have aged into any of these things, but it had seemed possible to me then, sitting in the foyer, which was off-white and taupe and underground. The man draped a sweater over his shoulders and moved through the museum absently while guards sat on high black chairs. Soon the man would be gone and it would be me again, as though in a tasteful underwater tomb. When the man paused between galleries, I asked him what he thought of the collection, though it wasn't my habit to speak to people I didn't know.

He said that he had once worked for the museum, and had been in charge of raising funds for its construction, though he hadn't ended up liking it, and he took some responsibility for that. He no longer reminded me of my father, but I was struck by this, that a man who reminded me of my father had turned out to be the man who'd created the building where I had sat for so many hours. When I went into the bathroom, I found myself wishing I had asked his name, and I felt the loss of him, that we might never see each other again.

I saw him a week later. On my way home I had wandered off track and gotten lost. I did this often—I would leave the subway and walk in the direction opposite to where I was supposed to go. Sometimes I imagined a person watching me from up high—starting off in one direction before taking another, my misdirection gradually turning to panic—and imagined how different I must look from the other people on the street.

That day, after realizing I was lost, I was sitting on a bench and reading a newspaper, trying to orient myself, when the man walked by. I followed until he went into a restaurant called Delmonico's. He sat alone before a middle-aged brunette in a blouse and skirt joined him. She had smooth dark hair that shone in the light. The restaurant had white tablecloths and lanterns on the tables and windows that must have opened to the street but were closed then. I stood outside watching through the window until I finally went inside for a glass of wine.

Something in them moved me. They didn't seem romantic—he didn't try to touch her and didn't lean toward her—but sad, as if they had come to an end of something, but didn't know what it was. After their meal they left together, but they separated at the subway. When the train came, I got on with her. She closed her eyes, her body swaying with the movement. I sat close, closer than I should have, but I found I wanted to be near her.

The next day it rained and I crossed to the diner and found a table near a window. I read a novel about a woman who loved a priest who also loved her, but mostly they were kept separate, and she spent years alone on the prairie. When I returned, my boss said there was a woman who had asked for me but left without waiting for me to return. I felt it was the woman from the restaurant and was upset to have missed her. She had seemed like a gentle person.

Someone had once taken a chair from my table at a café. I had stood to get another chair. The change—the unexpected loss of the chair—had upset me, but then I was upset at myself for having to wander the café for another chair, while the others sat in a happy group, playing chess. After, I had used the chair to rest my feet, as if to explain my behavior. Do you feel this way? I would ask the woman. And, if she seemed kind and gentle enough, I might have asked her if we had to continue on.

How long do we do this? I would ask, thinking that, if there was a set time, it might feel possible.

The security guard's name was James. He was young and overweight and dressed sloppily. His Polo shirt was stained by the Big Gulp he kept on the counter, which was surprising in the austere museum. I first met him when a man came in who resembled a known art thief, and I was taken back to the room and shown a tape of my interaction with him. I couldn't remember the moment, but there it was, replayed for me. James told me that I didn't move much. He pointed toward the screen that showed the empty chair, the counter, and said there was a time when he had turned the monitor on and off because he thought it was broken, but then I had thrown something away.

After that we hung out from time to time. We would sit at the diner and talk about movies we had both seen, and sometimes I would watch tapes in the security room with him. I found it comforting that my time there had been recorded, that there were no lost moments, that I could think of a moment and find it again. Yet, when I played the tape from the day the woman came in asking for me, I didn't recognize any women in the footage. I kept playing the tape, searching. James pointed and expressed appreciation of the skirt that I had worn that day. You don't understand, I told him.

One day, after work, I found frames behind the museum Dumpster. One still had a painting in it, so I took it and crossed the street with it. The diner waitress was outside smoking. What is that? she said, bending down, her hair falling across her face. She said it reminded her of a print she'd had as a child. It had been over the sofa. It was washed-out greens and pinks, the colors of Monet, but even hazier. She looked back into the diner to see if anyone needed her, but there were only a few tables, everyone with head bowed.

I hung the painting in my apartment and found that other people repeated what the waitress said, that it reminded them of something they'd had as children. Eventually, I learned it was a print of a children's book cover, while I had begun to think we had all gone somewhere in a dream together. Her gaze had gone soft looking at the painting. She didn't seem to want to look away, in the way that shy people can have while examining things at parties. Is that why shy people are so curious? A life spent looking at things until the things themselves become interesting, until you have to see the bookshelves at parties, the small paintings outside bathrooms, all these places feel forbidden, but in fact everyone is right around the corner, and when someone passes you smile and try to leave, or they try to leave. But what other choice do we have? Sometimes that is the only consolation, that there's never been another choice.

Carrying the painting, I ended up at a bar in a neighborhood I didn't know. The streets were soft and tree-lined and narrowed to horizons that you could never reach. It was the kind of day when bars had drink specials listed on chalkboards outside, and this one also had large windows made of colored glass. Inside, there was a man from Peru who spoke faintly and several times pointed at the windows, asking me if I saw something. I didn't know what he was pointing at, whether it was something that had just passed the window, or something that was outside that was interesting to him, or whether he liked the windows, the colors of them and what they made of the world outside.

I remembered other cities I had visited. How difficult it

would have been to live in those places, and how difficult it was to be a stranger in a city. When you travel it is the same—first you know one street, then you learn another, then you go someplace else, until the city unfolds in your mind. I didn't take steps to learn how to find the bar again and didn't remember the name. Perhaps I like the magical qualities of not being able to find a place again. The Elentine or something. The small elephant.

I was worried back then, not that something bad was about to happen, but that it already had only I hadn't realized it yet. I rode the train on days when the museum was closed. I watched women—thin, spare, alone-looking women who were older than me, always carrying parcels, bags, overstuffed leather purses. The light did something to their faces, laid them bare. As if on trains they wore the faces they had when alone. One day I saw a woman who looked like the one from the restaurant. She was standing on the platform. But I couldn't tell, and I worried I was losing this, too. Losing my ability to identify a person. She stayed on the platform when the train arrived, watching it depart, made smaller by the distance we traveled from her.

During my last week at the museum, we put in a tape labeled "Gallery Five." I had never seen this gallery before. The tape showed a badly lit space. It was so dark that you couldn't see the art, only shapes on the wall and people walking toward them. On my third time watching, I identified the man and woman from the restaurant. I had overlooked them at first, as they were younger in the footage. The man had been wearing a hat and the woman was slimmer and moved in a lighter way.

The man was animated in a way he wasn't when I'd met him, and I wouldn't have been able to place him had I not taken out a recent tape to compare. What are you doing? James asked, before turning back to watch another monitor. He had little interest in what I was doing. The older version of the man, there he was, looking much like a man lost in a dream. That might have been why he had reminded me of my father, who would watch my brother and me playing on the floor, or by the woods, or near the sea with the same look, as if he had already left us.

The younger version of the man wasn't like this. He moved quickly and reached back to help the woman move through the crowd. He turned from time to time to speak to someone, lean in, shake hands. And then an image made me pause the tape so abruptly that James looked over. I saw, in the way that we always know ourselves—even in a photograph from an age we have no memory of—myself as a child.

I was only visible for a few seconds as I walked toward the man, touched him to steady myself, then walked back, not haltingly, or in any way lost. This certainty was so perplexing that I doubted if the child was really me, in the way that we sometimes wonder, when in love, whether this might be a person we don't love at all. It was only that I so rarely walked toward something without fearing it would disappear or prove not to be the thing I thought. On the tape, I walked like those people always passing me by. What had filled me with such certainty? When I, for all I could see of the footage, was so alone, little more than a speck, there for a moment, then lost for eternity, neither going somewhere nor coming from somewhere?

You could see all of us—the woman from the restaurant, the man who had reminded me of my father—all of us altered by what had happened, and yet there was no way to know what had taken place. All that was left was a man, surprisingly nervous and eager, sharing a smile with a woman who was not in any way memorable, missing the sadness—the way she had watched the train depart as if watching what she wanted most in life move away from her—that had made her so beautiful to me.

MAUREEN

Or another Portland story, one of those heard and almost forgotten, told late at night, when no one has anywhere to be and you're not sure if anyone is talking. Maureen had been the bartender at the Regency Bar for nearly twenty years. The place was under the highway ramp, and had dark wood, torn covers in the booths, and old lamps, though this wasn't lovely in the way this might suggest, just generic. Most of the men drank Bud from bottles and sat for a long time, and sometimes, on slow nights, Maureen would lean over and talk to them. She had been beautiful when she started, and most of the men could remember that. One night she told them about being at the beach with the man she had once been married to and their baby daughter. It was easy to see a younger Maureen on the shore, wearing a stretched-out bathing suit and cutoffs, her long hair greasy but shining. Already some of the weight gained, but it would have looked good on her. There would have been something sympathetic in the thickening under her arms. And her husband, thin and bare-chested, a mustached man spread across the blanket, with their baby playing in between. The two of them drinking cups of beer, and afterward walking barefoot through the parking lot, teetering on pavement embedded with small rocks. The shock of the hot car, then lifting the baby in and buckling her, careful not to clip the fat of her legs.

That baby had died later, a few years later, in a car accident. Maureen had been newly divorced when it happened. She had just moved into the apartment and her ex came on Saturdays to pick up the girl, Clarice. That morning Maureen could tell he had been drinking, but still, she helped her daughter into her coat and went back upstairs. She enjoyed the empty apartment. She would do nothing—pick up laundry, smoke a cigarette, take a bath. She had been lying in bed, watching the curtain, smelling her shoulder, when the phone rang.

After that time, she felt there was something wrong with her, that she was empty in ways she shouldn't have been. That emptiness prepared her for what she saw on the town green one day, years later—a little girl who looked like her daughter, in a group with other children, being led down a path. She looked to see if anyone else noticed, thinking perhaps they were an imaginary thing that had come to fill the space. But other people, too, saw the children.

The next time, she followed them to story time at the library. She stood outside the children's room in the basement, watching the kids, then went to the information desk and asked if she could read. Well, the woman said, it's usually the librarian or someone at the senior center, but we always like help here. So on Tuesdays she put on her good dress, a thin spring dress she had owned for years, and brushed her hair while watching the old man in the garden out her window, the old man working his tomato patch in a green hat, moving over the earth like a delicate animal. She didn't look at him when she backed out of the drive, but felt he knew.

Afterward, after reading at the library, she would smoke by the fence and try not to get too close to what was happening. She felt if she moved smoothly enough, without sharpness or rise in her voice, if she didn't pay attention, or look closely, only watched from the corner of her eyes . . . The few times she approached the girl were an allowance. Did you like that book? she had asked her. What she must have seemed to the little girl, with her off-voice and stifled insistency. She wasn't in control, but felt if she moved slowly, almost crept, that nothing would startle and break loose.

When her ex-husband appeared at her door one day, she thought it was a harbinger, the very thing she was trying to avoid. It reminded her of the Saturdays when he had picked up their daughter. Opening the door was like that, too, except he was older and it hadn't done well for him. It was as if they had agreed on this play, but their aging and lack of reason made it a pitiful thing. She looked past him to see if the man was in the garden, but she didn't see him. What do you want? she asked her ex-husband. He held up his hands, Just to talk to you. She asked him to wait while she put on shoes. Upstairs she tied her raincoat, put on flats. She looked out the bathroom window for the old man but still didn't see him and wondered if that was a bad omen.

They walked to the corner bar, slipping inside the door. They stood near each other. It was midday and nearly empty. He was more lost than she was. It occurred to her that he was drunk, but she couldn't tell. Do you still drink the same? she asked. He offered to get it, but she thought he might not have money, and said, No, I'll get it, find us a seat. He picked a booth along the side wall; tinted windows showed a yellowed version of the empty street. She bought one drink and sat at the edge of the seat, sliding it to him.

I'm sorry, he said. I didn't think of what I would say. He wrapped his hands around the glass. Instead of looking at his face, she looked outside. It was raining, what looked like yellow rain on a darker yellow sidewalk. I'm getting married again, he said. We're going to move to Florida. I'm going to start up a bar there. He waited for her to say something. She said that she had to go. He reached for her, but she slid from the booth.

On the sidewalk, she put a hand in her purse and fumbled with her cigarettes. She lit one, threw it down, walked back to the bar. She stood in the entryway. There was a man in the far booth where they had been. He was tall, lanky, dark haired. She took steps toward him, but his features aligned into those of a stranger's.

During her shifts she often smoked to steady herself. You could see her out there, holding her sweater closed with one arm and turning away from the wind. She looked like those women you find in rural areas who have kids, do the cooking, and work, who have no femininity in them, but also nothing hard, it was just that life had brought them to having no extra gestures.

NASHUA

When I travel, I often visit another town nearby, someplace I wouldn't otherwise go. Nashua, I think, was like that. It was after Christmas and I was watching, for a time, a teenager and two dogs for a family west of Boston. I rarely saw the teenager, except to drive her from place to place, but I let the dogs out and walked them and picked up the garbage they had strewn about. I cooked meals I found in the freezer—shrimp, individual-sized lasagna. The house was large enough that cleaning people came every few days, and, when I couldn't find something, I always thought that the cleaning people had moved it when I had probably just forgotten where it was. One night I drove to an old, unheated cinema to watch a musical. It involved driving unknown roads in the snow and then driving back, hoping I would find the teenager at home, chasing the dogs, trying to get them in their cages. There was, as always, the relief of living within a life that wasn't mine, of raising the heat and walking barefoot across the bathroom's stone floor.

Around this time, I realized I had fallen in love again, this time with a man who was a drinker. I remembered a story by Alice Munro in which a woman, sensing she is falling in love, and fearing what had happened the other times, gets in a car and starts to drive and keeps on going. It was a snowy day when I thought about this and I sat in my bedroom and imagined waiting it out, how long it might take. Outside there was the scrape of shovels. But for what other reason are we alive? I thought.

I had driven to Nashua from Boston to look for farmhouses. I was researching abandoned farmhouses and wanted to find a part of New Hampshire with both rural and urban poverty. Once there, I bought a bottle of whiskey at the tax-free shop, then found the Salvation Army. I bought fabric to make curtains and asked the woman behind the register about directions, but she knew the roads by different numbers than were listed on my map.

As I drove the hills, the sun hit low across an apple orchard and it was so striking that it didn't surprise me to see an abandoned farmhouse—just like that, just what I was searching for—at the top of the hill. I pulled over and started to walk. There was a neighborhood watch sign nailed to a tree, and I thought of the neighbors watching me in the snow.

Through the window I saw furniture, not arranged to make the room habitable, but grouped together as if to be taken away. It wasn't a beautiful farmhouse—it was in the style of a musty-looking ranch—or I would have felt the desire to go inside. I was glad the desire was less than it might have been. Still, it was hard to leave, and below the hills I stopped at a church. The door to their secondhand shop opened, but the woman inside said that it was closed, that I would have to come back the next day.

• • •

There was a time in my life when several poets I knew gave me their poems, and one man—who I didn't think was a very good poet otherwise—gave me one that I still have. He wrote about being in a hotel in France and never going out, and overhearing the woman in the neighboring room telling her lover about him, saying that seeing him was like seeing a man at the end of a long tunnel. Some people, I took the poem to mean, are lost already.

I thought of this poem when I went to Poland to find the village my grandparents had emigrated from. I never made it to the village and instead stayed a week in a small hotel off a village square—my room overlooked it—and I would sit in the window and smoke and watch pigeons. In the afternoon I'd go out for a doughnut and a cup of tea and walk around until it was time for an early dinner, and then I'd return to the hotel to read and drink from bottles of wine I had purchased near the train station. It was bad wine and I didn't drink much of it, but the wine in the hotel bar was worse.

I cried some nights as I wanted a child back then and I was almost past the point of being able to have one. I imagine that's why I was in Poland, because I wanted time to think about these things, such as this man and the poem he had written, and the little girl I might not be able to have. Seeing a ghost, having your own ghost, being the man at the end of a long tunnel, makes you into a ghost, too, separates you from the people around you. This town in Poland turned out to be a destination for schoolchildren, as Copernicus had once lived there, and his house had been made into a museum. The children came in packs. The streets near the museum were narrow and stone and winding, and I would come upon them, fifteen or twenty children in their winter coats, and always one or two tall, thin women behind them. They would pass and I would spend the rest of the afternoon walking, sometimes stopping at a café to write a letter. I was thinking of Warsaw, of going back to Warsaw, of avoiding the reconstructed city and instead walking the old streets outside of the center, but I never left that small town.

• • •

Though I feared I was falling in love with this man, the one who was a drinker, little happened between us. The nights we were around each other would softly fade out. He wore, all spring, winter, and fall, a caramel-colored wool coat with a belt around the middle that he wore untied. He was tall, with sandy-brown hair he kept at his chin. But it was the coat you remembered. I once, when waiting to board a bus, stood behind an older black woman. Her coat was a lot like Ansel's. It looked as if she had owned it her whole life, as if she had never been without it. She was not stylish—she wore sweatpants and a pair of walking shoes and a polyester scarf around her hair. It was as if the beauty of the coat had happened by accident. She tied it snug to her middle like a bathrobe.

Where did you get your coat? I asked Ansel once. We were drinking midday next to the window in an otherwise dark bar. A wood bench ran the length of the room. He waved his hand in the air, as if to say, who knows. The sun came in and I touched the wool. The question dropped in the way most did back then, not that the effort wasn't worth it—the effort of conveying information to each other—but that the moment had changed and the question wasn't there anymore.

Perhaps much of what drew us together was the way life felt to us. My memory was poor, and I had developed the habit of writing the names of things in a small notebook. I had put off doing this, as I worried it would become obsessive, but it got so that I couldn't remember a book I had just read, or an art exhibit, or a movie that touched me. A friend had screened a beautiful art film with footage of a snowy cabin north of New York. It alternated with shots of the city. Afterward, I couldn't recall the name of the film or the artist. Or another time, I was talking to a student and asked if he had seen *Sans Soleil,* and then, seeing nothing register on his face, I asked in a flurry—But that's a movie, yes? As if I had become worried it was a cleaning product.

Ansel's memory changed, too. When I was with him, I knew he would remember the moments differently the next day, but there was no way to know in what way, or what his consciousness—when drunk—what his consciousness felt like. I thought of that forgotten art film, with that clicking of a reel running, of the lights flickering at the end, of the moments when two films played over each other.

• • •

One night, after being at a bar with Ansel, I dropped him off at his apartment and he tripped on the stairs going up. It was painful to watch so I looked away. I drove from there to a diner on the corner that had recently opened and sat with a cup of tea. The waitress kept asking if I was okay. She was a kind girl whose parents were from India. Her shift was thirteen hours, from 8:00 p.m. to 9:00 a.m. Few people came in during those hours, and fewer people were likely to come, as the owner had fired the night cook earlier that week.

Ansel had wanted me to tell him about the diner, so I paid careful attention and tried to think of what I would say. It was a desperate thing being there. At a certain point I started to cough, bent over at the table. I must not have looked well. I hadn't taken my coat off. The waitress had teased out the jobs I held, and they were good jobs. She must have wondered what had brought me to such a place at three in the morning.

I never understood why Ansel drank like that. He would drink until he was falling down. In a sense I was magnetized, drawn in, and he must have known that. It seemed the cruelest thing to ask, so I never did, but I wondered if he knew that he did it, and if so, if he understood why. For some reason I had his apartment in my imagination, in the sense that I was able to picture it even though I had never been inside. We used to describe things to each other—details about our furnishings, the style of blankets we used, the layout, how we had set things up. There was one night—in all the time I knew him—when I went home with him. I thought I knew the tradeoff I was making, but I later learned that I was wrong, that I hadn't known what would happen or what it would feel like to be inside his apartment, or even what his apartment would look like.

• • •

After that, we rarely saw each other. It happened slowly. At first because he avoided me, and then later because it was too difficult—almost impossible—to have a drinker like that in your life. That summer my mother visited me in the city. We were walking down the street when a man who looked like Ansel walked by. I said his name, once, twice, and then, just when I was about to give up, my mother said his name more sharply. Still, he didn't turn. At the stoplight, he rounded the corner, and I walked into the crosswalk to try from there, but this man held his body so that I never saw his face. Later I decided it was both him and not him. My mother would sometimes bring it up. She wanted me to ask, but since I felt both versions were true, there was nothing to learn from asking him. It was a way to hold something—the memory of him—lightly enough so that all possibilities were true, and to not crush anything by asking if I loved him or not, and, if I loved him, trying to understand why.

STRANGERS

The only grocery store on the island was closing. It had been closing for a while, but no one said much about it, because no one saw a point in guessing at what you couldn't know. That's what people said if someone brought it up, mentioning how the shelves were nearly empty, or what someone had overheard someone else saying. Doesn't do much good guessing at it, someone would say. When what's going to happen is going to happen anyway. Some people on the island had given in to it, but others understood the beauty of those shelves winnowing down. That what it required would be nothing short of the New England stoicism so little required now.

Gene toed a box aside. He put items carefully in his basket. He didn't get too close to the rotting vegetables. At the checkout the woman told him it was official. I guess we've been figuring that, he said, bagging while she checked.

We'll have to get groceries on the mainland now, she said.

Suppose that's the only way, he said.

He paid, then handed the plastic bags to his grandsons to carry to the truck while he went around back to see if anything had been thrown out that he might want, but the Dumpster was nearly empty. The kids were already in the truck when he returned, so he got in and started it. He liked to look over while he drove—at the way the wind went through their hair, at the broken-down toughness of the truck—but he never said anything about it. What they must have thought of him, though they probably didn't think much about him, probably just thought of him as a permanent thing.

It was a Thursday so their mother was coming the next day from the mainland. He tried to think of what he hadn't found at the store to tell her to pick up, but it always seemed they got along just fine. Though she'd notice and say, There's no orange juice for them, and what could you say to that? Seems they're doing fine without orange juice, he'd say. She was always tired, seemed to him nothing was needed more than anything else.

At home the kids stayed outside and he put the groceries away, putting the plastic bags under the sink to use as trash bags. Kneeling, he found it hard to believe that there would be an end to these bags. He had been using them for as long as he could remember and thought they were always going to be there.

Their mother came over on the afternoon ferry. You look tired, he said when she got in the truck.

I'm fine.

I'm sure you're fine, but that doesn't mean you don't look tired.

She turned, the light hitting her hair in a soft way, changing the amber to pink. I had a hot dog before the ferry, she said. It was terrible. Sort of wonderful, but terrible, too.

He liked picking her up when it was just him. He remembered when he used to wait for girls when he was young, and if they were beautiful, and you were sitting by the ferry, and there were boats and birds when they came, it felt full of hopefulness. He told her the boys were next door at Bea's. They like it there, she said, the horses and chickens. We should at least get them a cat.

She had missed the morning ferry because she had fallen asleep after breakfast in the attic room she rented on the mainland for half the week. She wondered what was becoming of her. It wasn't what she had anticipated when she took the job the month before, the way she felt in the morning with the window open and the ocean, seeing a sliver of it in the distance. It was the foghorn that woke her to find she had missed the ferry. She had a little rice and pickles, and ate on the kitchen floor, then called Gene. That's fine, he had said. There'll be some quiet for you. I've had so much quiet, she said. Everyone thought of how exhausted she must be and how she would need time to adjust, but they didn't think of how she was alone in a room most of the time. The week before she had gotten a library card and taken out a stack of movies. She watched two the first night, liking how a movie lights a dark room. She left the popcorn bowl on the floor, and in the morning sat on the sofa, which was a wool plaid that gave the back of her legs a rash, and ate the popcorn with her coffee, then smoked a cigarette.

When they reached the house, Gene got her bag from the truck and she went inside to wash up, then they had a drink on the patio. Angelo's is closing, he said.

I guess it will be easier for us because I can bring stuff over, she said.

Her back had a slight bend to it, and her shoulders hunched

forward. She wasn't quite so beautiful as she was quick, the way her thoughts carried her forward, even though you didn't know what she was thinking most of the time. She pushed her bare feet in front of her and leaned back in the chair. They watched off in the distance, but different distances.

After the drink she changed into her bathing suit, then walked to pick up the boys while Gene went inside to think over dinner. He thought of how there weren't vegetables and he was going to have to do a good job of covering up this fact. He had tried to grow a garden several years ago and found he was ineffectual, that he was only good at immediate things and that the vegetables, when not grown yet, were difficult for him to worry over. He walked down the street to the stand for corn and tomatoes. When Meghan and the kids came back he had the corn boiled and the tomatoes sliced thin on a plate with salt and pepper on them.

When Meghan returned to the mainland, she changed quickly after work then went to the Wharf, a restaurant along the pier with an outside bar. Women there were not very pretty, though there was something to them, with their skin so tan you felt if you pressed your finger the mark would stay for a long time. She wondered if their breasts were the same color. They wore cheaply made clothes that might not have been inexpensive, thin white pants, tank tops with straps that braided and crossed in back. Oddly straight hair. What this place must require of you, she thought. Her shoulder-length hair lifted and curled in the humidity, and she'd taken in her clothes herself. She looked the same as she did ten years ago. There was no style at all.

She kept her handbag at her feet, thought of the beauty of the island and wondered why that wasn't enough to make you want to stay. When she took the job, people thought she'd find another husband, and then would move the children to the mainland. She looked at the men at the bar and imagined one of them as that husband. It seemed a funny thought now, even though she had thought, at first, that it was likely, as she would be working at the hospital. But she had found that the men at work had wives, or there was something off about them. She hadn't accounted for the hardness in the people who were left, like her, without someone.

She sat near a wood column at the corner of the bar. It was made of driftwood. There was a net-and-driftwood design here that wasn't on the island. There was no need there to remind yourself you were living on the water. A man put his hand along her back so as not to bump into her. When she turned, his face was hard, and he had the same skin, and his hair was lightened by the sun, and he had on a collar shirt. They all looked as if they had gone golfing, or like they had become middle school teachers because that's the job you could find and it meant summers off, though their imagination hadn't given them much of an idea for those summers.

There was a group of men who looked like teachers, and women in white pants across the bar, drinking heavily, and after a time one of the men separated and sat next to her. She thought she had come this time to start something with one of them, but when the man talked to her, she pressed her body back against the wood column.

She liked waiting for the ferry, liked the people waiting with coolers and old nylon packs that they'd been using for years. When the boat came, she stepped on and took a seat near the bow.

Gene was waiting on the island with the kids. The two

boys were sitting on the bench together, and he stood behind. She gave him the paper bag of groceries. All her things fit in a second bag. He asked that she start getting plastic for the groceries so they could use them as trash bags. They talked quietly of household things.

The next day they woke, had breakfast, then cleaned the house. They opened the back slider and she took out the chairs and looped curtains over the rods. He swept while she scrubbed the kitchen, scrubbing with her hair falling from its elastic, wearing yellow plastic gloves and a loose dress. He wore a flannel shirt and soft pants, and when he passed she could smell him. She had grown used to living with this gentle man.

They settled on the arrangement after her husband, his son, had left, and it was just her and the kids. Gene was living on the other side of the island. He could have been angry with her; he could have judged her. Everyone else did. They acted as if what happened belonged to the island, and wasn't something private. What had happened was almost nothing like what it looked like, but people never realize this.

When they had decided, not long after everything had happened, she had been in her living room. Gene had come over to the house. He sat down and asked if she wanted to stay on the island. She hadn't thought about it, and he said that she would want to think things over, that it might feel soon, but that she would need to think about it. If she wanted to stay here, then one of them would need to work on the mainland. He said that he would do it, and she could look after the kids, if she'd prefer that, but that it would probably be easier for her to get a job. He had talked quietly to her that day, and much of what they decided on ended up being exactly what they did, though at the time it hadn't felt real to her.

She had looked at Gene that day. He looked younger, different than he had looked before, when he was simply the father of the man she had married. He was a man who had become suddenly necessary, and that changes them. She said then, Do you want to know more about anything, for me to talk about anything, so that you know? Maybe another time, he said, that might be what happens, but right now we should focus on the smaller things, these things that are going to have to happen.

Now, months later, after they had cleaned the house and after the kids had gone to bed, they poured second drinks. Have you made any friends? he asked her.

God no, she said, and tried to explain how it was there. His shirt was rolled to his forearms, and the fabric was touching the wood of the table, and she thought this was what the table had been expecting all along, him to sit there.

Maybe it would be better if they lived on the mainland, too, he said. With you. If you all lived there full time. We want to keep this certain kind of life, but maybe after a while it just does harm.

She didn't understand his change, and said, I think that we should keep it this way right now.

She stood to get the radio from the living room. She plugged it in in the kitchen and turned the game on so low they could barely make it out. He continued with what he was saying, which was the intelligence of considering the mainland in not too long, six months, a year.

I don't want to think past this right now, she said.

Gene had, when his son left for college, never expected him to come back. When Shaun came back with a wife, and they had children, Gene realized that he was trying not to get close to them. He expected them to leave, so there had been a lot that he had missed, that maybe other people had known before him, because he had been thinking of his own survival. He had imagined them both there and not there, so he would be able to continue on without them, and felt he had to understand that they could go and do what's often done—send Christmas cards from Connecticut with pictures of the kids, or those postcards people are always putting on their fridges. The realization of his daughter-in-law's inner life had been slow to materialize, had not really started until four months before, on the day she came up his drive alone. He had come out of the house, wiping his hands on a cloth. She wasn't one for agitation, and she looked around as if she had misplaced something. He was thought commendable in the way he handled the situation, but he knew how useless he had been, trying to preserve himself as if he were anything to think of, when he was just an aging man inside his house, trying to fix a sink. A braver man would have been willing to sacrifice his happiness before that point, seeing as his happiness, and himself, were the slightest things.

She had fallen in love with another man, and her husband had disappeared with the kids. She thought they were still on the island, though, as the ferry captain hadn't seen them. This is a lot to take in, he had said to her. Well, what should we do? he said. It was uncommon to be standing there, united in this sudden way. We could go over to Matt's, he said. Matt was the island manager. No, she said, let's not do that. Why? he said. Just not him, she said. Anyone but him. I see, he said, thinking that it would have been easier if the man she had fallen in love with wasn't also the man in charge of the island. Well, he said, we'll go, and you'll stay in the truck.

Matt's office was in a low cinder-block building, with the ferry office to one side and the administrative offices on the other. Matt had thick black hair, was himself a thick, strong man. Gene thought of what loneliness could do to you, that Meghan had been lonely in ways no one else had thought of, but this man had.

If he had to pick between knowing all this and not knowing, he would pick the moment when he was fixing his sink, insulated from them, thinking of how he would get cards from them, and that he would grow older alone, that you couldn't guess at how isolated the self was, and that was what getting old could sometimes be, that it becomes quiet enough to hear it in yourself. But during the ride to Matt's he learned that his son, who worked in a school on the mainland, had found out about the affair and gone desperate with love for his wife. Gene didn't understand this way of taking things and wondered where his son had discovered it. Gene would have left his wife and met someone else in time. There was comfort to find everywhere. Gene wondered if it was love for her or just desperation with life. They always looked so much the same. Why do we think we can't live without a certain person? Then there are others who don't think this way. He couldn't begin to understand why his son had taken the children. Maybe he thought if he ran away by himself no one would try to find him.

After talking with Matt, Gene had driven with Meghan to the World War II bunker facing the open ocean. They parked near the scrub, then walked through the dunes, then stood there, listening. He jumped down and she came after, and they stood in the space with the sudden surprise of windows overlooking the water. She looked out the windows, as there was no sense in looking further for the kids. It was clear enough they weren't there. Well, you learn quickly when looking for something that it isn't there, and that you're going to the very places you won't find it. For instance, if you lose something in your house, you'll search the same place over and over again, because it has stopped mattering where you look.

They looked next in the abandoned cottages, then went to the homes of people they knew.

On the second night they went home and she fell asleep on the sofa while he waited up. If she had been awake when the kids appeared through the front door, she could have greeted them while he ran to find his son, but in that moment when he had the choice, he picked his grandsons, picked to lower himself so he could see their eyes and try to calm them. Then she woke and he went outside but it was too late. They had spent two days looking even though they knew they wouldn't find them; this time he admitted there was no sense in trying to find his son. Gene put the front light on and went back to his grandsons and daughter-in-law.

He had been with them since, been with her, except for when she was on the mainland. This had unintended consequences. You grow to love a woman, seeing her that way, the way she comes through the back door in her bare feet, or the way her cheek looks when she turns and there is a soft slope. If you live closely and there's peacefulness between you, and she has something pretty in her features or movement, you're naturally going to feel love for her, or want to protect her. He had understood this. But he hadn't expected what it would feel like when she was away, that the feeling of everything else went away, too, or how he would try to practice, during the days she was there, her going away, so that it wouldn't come as a shock, or hurt when it happened.

Sometimes when he went back to the house he thought he might find his son as he had been, not toward the end, but before the kids, a distant man puzzled by his surroundings. Island life didn't prepare you for any other life, and there had been the breakdown in college. Gene had gone to Boston to visit Shaun. He remembered his son slumped on his dorm bed, his legs sprawled out, with no determinate shape to his tall, thin body. Gene had sat at the edge of the bed, unsure of what to say. Breakdowns were not in their vocabulary, and he had not thought of it that way, though the knowledge of it had come later, that it wasn't going to come back again, how his son had been. It's true, there's something broken afterward, no matter what everyone says. On the island mostly it was alcoholism, which he wished Shaun had been able to muster instead, as he would have been able to survive in that way, he would have been able to hobble along with some degree of cheer, but this fragility left him no match for anything. Gene sat at the edge of the bed. Are you telling me you won't go to your classes? he asked him. When Shaun didn't answer, he said, Well, what do we do then? I guess we withdraw you from school, and then you and I go back? I'd rather stay here, his son said. Gene decided to go to the market to get things for the dorm fridge, which then involved cleaning out what had gone bad. He bought apple juice and poured Shaun a cup. I'm having trouble understanding this, he told his son, I'm trying, but I'm having trouble.

He woke to his son shaking and didn't understand at first

that his son was trying to cry without making a sound. Where does your roommate go? Gene asked him. To his girlfriend's. It was a series of things that he didn't think would affect the future. It hadn't occurred to him that it would last inside his son. Shaun had come back and spent the summer landscaping on the mainland, and the work had been good for him, slowed him so he was able to finish school the next year, and he stayed in Boston, and met his wife, and they came back to the island and had children. When his son had disappeared after taking the children and returning them unharmed, Gene was able to tell Meghan about the time in college. He told her about holding Shaun's hand. He rarely touched his son, but after three days he'd found himself so exhausted that he reached for him. He said that what she did with Matt would have been painful, but that it hadn't been the reason Shaun had left, that it had come out of another time, from events that occurred before Shaun had met her. And you have your sons and this is your life now, he said. If Gene hadn't understood him that week in Boston, years later at least he was able to understand that it was sad and that was all. I can't get over it, Meghan had said. We stop trying to think that way, he said. We think about what we're going to do instead.

Now his son wasn't at home, and Meghan was on the mainland again. He had the kids wash up, then he read to them. After, he sat in the living room with a beer. Bea came over, and they sat on the front step. They had been romantic, but this had stopped months earlier. At a certain point he hadn't wanted her to come over, so he had been going to her place, but that had stopped, too. She had come over that night because she knew Meghan was gone. Bea had pale, thin skin, and soft white hair.

She grew herbs that she made tea with. During the times when he had gone over, she would drink tea while he drank beer. Now the field below was lit with fireflies, though not as many as the month before. Beyond that, you could feel the sea. She said, It seems that you're not coming over anymore.

It's been a while, he said.

Anywhere else, she said, that would be how it was, there'd be little sense in mentioning it. But here, she said, we get so few chances at anything, and so I wonder why. He thought of the isolation that she, because of him, would now experience, but didn't feel it. Not in any part of him, not sympathy in any part of him for her.

And then I knew why, she said, and I wondered why it had ever seemed important to me to know why. Why had it?

When she left he watched her walking in the thick air, her white blouse lit by the moon, like she was a spectral thing moving away from him. But what good is there in keeping the things you don't want, simply because they are something?

He turned off the front lights, put his glass in the sink. Went to the hall so he could see into the kids' room, see that they were still there. He had held himself together and what good had it done? For whose benefit had he held himself together? Certainly not for anyone else's, but not really for himself, either.

Gene remembered his exaltation when he finally left his son. How he'd fiddled with the radio in the truck to get a song, and rolled down the windows, and stopped for a nice dinner off the highway, then slept in his truck until the ferry came in the morning. It had been good to be home, to have slipped out from under something. He had called his son and felt stronger talking to him, more able to help. If we leave someone and feel better, we let ourselves think we have done the right thing. Of course it's not true, he now knows, taking off his boots, lying on his bed, the blankets with their moist smell of the island.

In the morning he took the kids to Bea's. She had put out stuff to make boxed muffins. She had done this with them before, and they had liked how inside the box there was a can with blueberries. It was a simple thing to have liked, but they had liked it. He stood there while they went down the hallway. Eventually they would leave, or he would leave. They couldn't stay like this forever. The night before on the steps, Bea had talked about his son. We weren't that close, our families, she had said. But still, when he was young, and I would be on my porch at night, it must have been after your dinner, I could always count on him coming out the back door, and the minute he got out, he always started to run, usually down the field, as if it was something just being outside. It was a terrible thing, what happened, she said. The way he disappeared. I didn't know what to say after. I wanted to tell you that. That I wanted to say something but didn't know what to say.

She had spoken quietly, in the dark, while they had both looked ahead at the field. He lay in bed afterward trying not to think of it. He thought of how they had found the house where his son had taken the kids, where they had stayed for two days. How it was small and brightly lit, and there were blankets there still, and a few of his son's shirts.

CITIES I'VE NEVER LIVED IN

During the trip, the lover I had left behind in New York had stopped calling. I was glad to be traveling, for the movement it gave me, but I was uncertain how my life would be when I got home. I didn't want another period of instability, and I felt the suspension you feel when you're fine, but you're worried it won't last, and there's nothing you can do to make it stay.

I had come up with the idea years before—when I first became interested in soup kitchens. I made the plan to travel the United States, going to small interior cities and going to kitchens there. I had volunteered in kitchens in the past and had found it comforting. I would work for a few hours and then would sign my name and get in line and eat, scrunched over, not poor enough to eat there if I hadn't worked, but not a volunteer doing it out of goodness. Lost, probably, in ways that made me more comfortable in places like those—the church halls, the Styrofoam plates, the trays, the gentle feeling of caretaking and cafeteria lines—and lost perhaps in ways understandable to those around me.

I didn't get far in the trip, however, before I became unsure why I was doing it. My first city was Buffalo and I arrived late, by train, taking a taxi to the hostel. The next day I walked to a mobile kitchen that was supposed to be parked outside the library at 7:00 p.m., but it was already gone when I arrived. I decided to stay an extra night so that I could go to the kitchen the next day, at the time the kitchen now arrived. The next day I stood in line to get the plastic bag that held dinner. A woman carried a box with more food—Baggies filled with granola bars and crackers—and people took those as she passed. When she came to me, I said that I only wanted the food there, pointing to where dinner bags were being passed down. I was surprised to hear my voice, that vulnerability that was of such little help usually, but it was honest in that line, honest and understandable. No, it's okay, the woman said gently, this is food, too. I took the bag of snacks, and, when it came time, took the plastic bag that held dinner.

I carried the food into the library. Holding the bags changed how I felt about myself. It made me feel more vulnerable or exposed or fragile. For a number of years I had been struggling to hold myself together, though I had worked to disguise this, and now carrying the thin bags made this visible, made people look at me. I walked around the library until I found the café. I asked the man working the register if I could eat there, and he said yes. Dinner was bland macaroni with tomato sauce and meatballs. There was also a turkey sandwich and cookies for the bus the next day.

After, I stood in the foyer. Windows overlooked the street where the mobile kitchen had been. It was gone now, and I felt the loss of it, as if I had not done it properly and wanted to try again. Others waited there. An older black man asked if I was waiting for a bus. No, I said. He then assumed I was waiting for a ride. No, I said, I'm just here.

I walked toward the hostel. It was overcast, rainy, and cold. The streets were mostly deserted. There was much about Buffalo that was difficult to put into words. It felt like a city that had been deserted and then, years later, been repopulated by the poor. Or maybe the poor had been in the city all along, but had waited to emerge. The main street was being ripped out and a metro ran through the rubble. Though the streets were deserted, there were always people in the metro car when it passed, so it felt like they, too, were leaving. All the metro stops—and there were many, every block or so along that street—piped music, and at first, walking the street, I didn't know where the music was coming from. Then the metro passed and disappeared under the street. One man on the sidewalk said to his friends, There goes our metro to nowhere.

What struck me most were the decorations: a sweeping arch over one metro stop, a gold globe on a roof, the opera hall sign that lit up six stories into the sky. This had once been another place. And the signs made me lonely because they were built for another time and for someone else.

I thought of the cab driver who had picked me up from the train at one in the morning. He said I would know him by the dice. His name was Ed. Ed's taxi service. He never turned around, just talked and drove facing forward. Blue light hit the sharp line of his cheek. I'd found that people who worked those jobs—the picturesque and hard jobs of the cities—were aware of what they were and were aware of what you were after, and often told stories as part of the service.

All drugs in here, he said as we drove through a boarded-up neighborhood. Last week a taxi driver, he said, in one of those white taxis you saw waiting by the train, was found murdered. It won't be solved. What someone does—someone who needs money—is hail them—the taxi drivers or pizza drivers, because they have cash with them—the drivers need to be making change, so they'll always have cash with them.

I imagined, as he talked, the fragility of those men, of Ed coasting through the quiet early morning, lit in blue. Got robbed one night, Ed said, then I became friends with a couple of black drivers to learn the tricks. Now you think about who to pick up, who not to pick up. He showed me where they were building the new houses, the new developments. All the old houses are past repair, he said.

Later, I read about the cab driver who had been shot and left in his backseat. Most articles were the same—giving the details of the death, and then the details of the funeral—but one writer interviewed several taxi drivers, calling them a close band of brothers. One man had rushed to the scene thinking it was one of his drivers, but it had been a different company. Another man talked about the additional security that people were calling for. He said that you could put in cameras, you could track the people, but in the end, the man in the article said, I walk in faith.

All day I sat in the lower bunk in my hostel, the only one in the room. A heating vent blew and from time to time I heard the sound of rain. Otherwise it was quiet. It was a relief whenever the vent turned on.

In Detroit I took a picture of a man on the street. I thought a lot about this. I wanted to take pictures of what I was seeing, but it didn't feel right. Poverty was everywhere and was overwhelming. People lived in this poverty, and this life was filled with details that I wanted to hold on to, but I found it was passing too quickly. I walked the outskirts of Detroit, and black men wandered past as if drifting or lost in the landscape. I sat and waited for buses and people came up to me. They said simple things—good day, or don't get hurt, or would I like a bag to sit on. Or they would ask if I knew where the Salvation Army was, or if I knew where the Greyhound station was.

In Cleveland, I was walking down a street filled with bistros and shops when a man hailed me. He was selling beauty products from a plastic bag and walked a block with me. He said he was from Detroit, but he meant Detroit Street in Cleveland. I bought bodywash for five dollars—a bottle of expensive, local bodywash—then he walked away. It occurred to me that I could have taken his picture. He had sadness deep in his face, but the surface of his face was buoyant, lit. It was too much to have the moment and then have the moment pass, and to be the only one who saw that face.

It was that way in Detroit when I passed a row of abandoned apartments near the hostel. Two long buildings faced each other across an empty field. White children played in the field, and parents stood in a sliver of doorway watching them. I wanted to take a picture, but I didn't want to disturb the quietness of passing them.

When I finally took a picture, it was of a man begging near Slows Bar BQ. I had eaten and was carrying leftovers. A man sitting in a lawn chair on the sidewalk told me to be careful, to not bump into the garden. He was in front of a brightly painted wall, and before I could ask, he said, You want to take a picture? He moved out of the way. At my hesitation he said, Or you want me in it? You in it would be nice, I said. As I took the picture, he energetically held up his sign. I wanted to tell him that he didn't have to do that, but instead I gave him change and asked, Do you mind that people take your picture? He said that he didn't. People want a picture of the homeless, he said. Then it was clear that he wanted me to move along.

In Detroit, I ate in the Capuchin kitchens. They ran two places. One served people in extreme need, mostly men, many homeless, and many with mental illness. The other fed working poor families, many with children. I picked the second kitchen, though it was an hour away on the bus. When I arrived for lunch, I was cold and shaken. I felt that fragile feeling again. There was no sign-in or token system. I walked right in—past a listing of places where you could get a free shower—and stood as volunteers passed my tray down. The last one set a drink on it and said it was real Coke. There were no open tables. I asked a man if I could sit at the table with him and he nodded yes. Many of the people there knew each other. In one corner hung a mix of Christmas decorations and St. Patrick's Day decorations, though all were green, as if to work for either holiday. Cartons of milk were piled on the table, and the man asked if I wanted them, and I said no, so he took them. I gave him my milk. Another man sat and said, I wish there was cheese on this. I said, I think there's cheese on it. He took a bite and said I was right.

Eventually another man sat next to the man with the milks, and they had a conversation about drugs, and pills, and Oxycontin, and where to get the different things. I looked at the people volunteering, at how hopeful and kind they looked, and at the thin, spare wood cross on the wall behind them, and also at the people eating, who were kind in their own way. I thought that those few people passing out food—with their hands in little plastic gloves, and their cross behind them—should not be our major defense against this kind of poverty; as a defense it felt hopeful, frail, and largely hidden.

Because I spent a lot of time on the street, I met other people who spent time on the street. If I was traveling between cities and had my suitcase, these people asked for money, which I tried to give each time. I felt I was giving a lot of money, but this money—a handful of change from the bottom of my bag, or a dollar bill from my pocket—didn't add up to much. I had bought the bodywash from the man on the street, so that was five dollars. But it was also the best bodywash I had ever used. It felt like honey that cleaned you instead of making you sticky. So there was five dollars, and maybe I had given out, to others, another ten dollars, so that was fifteen dollars. Many times I was blessed by the people I gave money to. In Detroit, I gave money to a man on the street and afterward thought he was asking for more. No, I said, that's what I can give right now. He said he was only saying thank you. He told me a story about a new kind of hearing aid, one so small that others can't see it. Do you get what I'm getting at? he said. Yes, I said, though I was looking at the gray building behind him and imagining a pale ear over it. Also, I was thinking of whether I could take a picture of him.

At the Chicago train station, a stand sold tacos for two dollars. I stood in line while a man asked people for money. He kept pointing to food and asking the cashier how much it was, and then looking at the money in his hand, which never amounted to enough. I gave him a dollar. I thought of how little

I was giving. I could have bought him what he wanted. Or, when I took that picture, in Detroit, of the homeless man, I could have given him the leftovers I was carrying, but I found I wanted them. More than a dollar would be giving money I felt I needed. Of course, none of this would add up or matter. Except that I didn't give people something that wasn't easy for me to give. I paid for my tacos and gave the man the change. Bless you, he said.

In Iowa City I walked through a park. It was warm, or the air wasn't warm, but the sun was. The night before, getting in by bus, was bitter. My throat had swollen and I felt weak, but at least it was warm enough now and nice to walk through the park. There was a sparsely attended fair going on. A man said something that I didn't understand and reached for my hand. He seemed to ask what it was, what this fair was, and I said I didn't know. He held on to my hand as I drew it away. Another man tried to get me to sign a petition, but I said I wasn't from there. There was a table to legalize marijuana, a banner on free speech, and a sign against surveillance, mentioning both drones and what I thought to be strip clubs.

I saw a couple sitting on a bench with a sign saying that they were homeless. I walked up and gave them a dollar and asked where they were from. They had come in from Wisconsin. The woman said that her sister's husband had just received two life sentences. They were surprised that I hadn't heard about it. The husband had lit the house on fire and his three boys had died. The wife had gotten out with third degree burns. I looked it up later, and it was true, and the wife's picture looked like the woman on the bench. They were both large and both had pale round faces and red hair. Articles said the husband was tired of not having money and had wanted to start over. There was also a baby, and the wife had saved the baby, but the husband had tried to put the baby back in the fire. I told the couple I was very sorry. I also wanted to take their picture and thought of that while I was listening, thinking about whether it would be wrong to ask.

I sat on the grass near them. It was nice to tilt my face toward the sun. But it was more than that. I hadn't asked for the story, and, given it, wasn't sure what to do. Increasingly, the sadness of the people I met was creating the fabric around me, and everyday life was beginning to recede, to lose meaning. In this world that was gaining meaning there were also churches. They were everywhere and grew in number as I traveled. I wanted to have faith so that I could go inside the churches, hoping they could balance the story of the fire, to be the other side of the story, but mostly I found the buildings beautiful and liked to look at them. I liked best the ones with other buildings attached, so that they went further, deeper into the unknown, creating a cluster of buildings like a small village. Then you had windows and buildings and courtyards to look at.

At the Salvation Army soup kitchen in Iowa City, a man invited me to attend church the next day to hear him play guitar. He wrote the church's name on a tag that I had ripped from socks I had just purchased. It had been difficult to keep socks clean. We were eating turkey tetrazzini. It was terrible. The man across from us said, The only entitlement you need is to know the god that loves you. I left quickly, while they were in conversation, not wanting to be drawn in, thinking I would see the man the next morning, but it would have meant walking three miles, and a cough kept me up much of the night, and so I didn't go.

It was a lonely time, and my trip had slowed enough so that I felt it. But what could I do? I couldn't continue on so fast, doing one city every few days. There weren't enough cities in the world to make me happy. My lover still wasn't calling. I was tired of soup kitchens. I wasn't sure what I'd ever wanted from them, but they were like the cities—simply the same thing, one after another. Sitting upstairs in the library in Iowa City, I looked down to see the homeless walking around the block holding signs. People passed without looking. The woman whose sister had been burned in the fire walked laps with her sign fastened around her neck as if she were a child, and there was something childlike in the roundness of her face. I thought of what it felt like to be near a shelter or kitchen in a city when food was about to be served, and suddenly people emerged, coming down alleys, moving out from behind buildings, walking slowly, in a drifting way, to that one spot, and they seemed sometimes like the dead, or people who had seen the dead.

• • •

For several nights I dreamed someone was lying close to me. In one dream, a man lay near me at a concert. In another, I was doing yoga in a crowded room and a man stretched behind me. In these dreams there was the comfort of the activity and then the presence and warmth of a man. This was in Omaha. My mother was with me. It was as if she had brought the dreams. Her close to me, and my desire for the kind of love you're supposed to have once you're no longer someone's child. There were jobs I wasn't getting, learning about them, uncertain of what I would do when I got back, and then walking Omaha with my mother. She drew close to me when we neared the homeless shelter. A woman rose from where she was sleeping on the sidewalk and walked in front of us. She kept looking back. We were making her nervous and I felt sorry. We passed a fenced-in courtyard with a man screaming. We continued past the shelter toward a church. It was a humble wood church with red trim. There was a door under the stairs with a sign that read Only One Lunch Per Person, Open 10–12. It was closed, and the next morning we were driving to Kansas. There was something in the places I kept leaving behind. I imagined staying and going inside, imagined the room I would enter. It was as if the rooms and my desire for them were gathering in me as I traveled.

In Kansas City, I went to the St. Paul's community breakfast. We ate in a sunny, high-ceilinged hall. Afterward, I looked through the doors into the church. Blue stained glass windows rose above the altar. Behind me, the breakfast line kept growing. It had been a good meal. A man came up and asked if he could talk to me. I thought that he might be involved with the church and, seeing the way I stared inside, might try to talk about God, but he was only asking me to dinner. Dinner seemed a fine offering to make to a woman eating breakfast at a soup kitchen, but I was leaving the next day.

Outside someone asked, Where is your man, where is your boyfriend?

I went to an exhibit on hunger at a county art museum in a Kansas town. The town's soup kitchen was in the center with a large sign that said Welcome to All. Many soup kitchens didn't have signs and weren't at the listed address, were instead set farther back, behind another building. In the exhibit in this town, the artist had taken pictures of people who had gone hungry and interviewed them. They had talked about their lives, about what the experience of going hungry had been for them. The artist had traveled for years working on the project. There were forty or fifty black-and-white portraits, each with the person's story told through headphones. I couldn't listen to all of them, so I picked people based on their faces. They talked about their lives, how they had become homeless, what that had felt like to them. I wanted to find someone intelligent, someone who would tell me something about being poor and lost. It was nice when they simply talked. Mostly I put headphones on to hear a voice, and to hear how they told a story, how they summarized an experience that must have been chaotic and something that still hadn't ended for them.

Afterward, I tried to explain to my mother that I was happy I went, though I didn't think it was effective art, as it was too compassionate. Can something be too compassionate? she asked. I said that art can end up being compassionate—because you're trying to communicate to people and that's a compassionate act—but making it is often unkind. Artists take images and stories from people without telling them, and artists are doing it for their own ends, or for the ends of art. Even if they have morals or set limits, they are still taking from people. Their interest in another's life is often for themselves. This artist didn't want to do this. He wanted to portray these people as they were, and, in that way, it was a good study, but I wanted more. I wanted to know how he saw these people. I wanted him to forget who they were.

The question started to become what was effective art about the hungry or the homeless, and there wasn't an answer. I took from everyone on the trip. I took meals and stayed for free with friends and strangers. I was patient and present with the poor—the people in the kitchens and on the street—but I was shut off with most others. I was tired after the kitchens. My openness meant someone always talked to me. There was a woman no one would go near. She sat next to me. She didn't touch her food. I kept eating. You're hungry? she said. The food is good, I said. When I stood, she hugged me, feeling her hands along the sides of my body.

I wasn't doing any good, I knew. I had liked the artist at the county museum, his description of hunger and his project, but I didn't think he thought he was doing good, either. He could have done more had he not been so faithful. They were only people after all. When you travel you see how many there are, how they fill whatever place you go to. It was hard to see the children in the lines. It wasn't hard to see the adults, but it was hard to see the children.

Later I dreamed that I was teaching again. That I was in a classroom with a circle of students. I hadn't been able to get a teaching job that year. In interviews I was vulnerable, scared, and trying to disguise this. I missed teaching. Missed being alone in a classroom with students, trying to do my best for them, which was, in the way those things often worked, never enough. When I got to St. Louis, I let myself into the apartment of a stranger who had hidden a key for me. I curled onto the iron bed in the spare room and called my lover. I told small stories about what I had packed, and about looking in the thrift store for a pair of lighter shoes and another shirt. It wasn't like me to repeat stories, but I kept repeating those. My mother had left the week before and I was more afraid than I had expected. He wanted me to come back. There were times when my stubbornness, my ability to press on, made life harder, when it would have been better to let things fall apart, to go home, and I wondered if the trip had become this.

I was thinking of King's bookstore in Detroit. How, when I walked in, the woman behind the register had said, Oh, you've been here before. When I said it was my first time in Detroit, she said, There's someone who looks just like you then. Hours earlier, when I was in the street, looking at a ruined theater, a man had stared at me, and said, You work at the restaurant? No, I had said. So I asked the woman behind the register if she knew anything about my double. Does she work at a restaurant? I said. She didn't know. She felt that I had been in many times before, and so hadn't explained how they organized the books.

I looked for the authors I always looked for, but they didn't have them. Instead, they had authors with the same last name. Looking for Denis Johnson—trying to find the old edition of *Jesus' Son*—I found ten other Johnsons, many of them women. It was the same with Walser. It was as if the famous authors didn't exist, and there were only the unknown versions. I found an old edition of a Thomas Bernhard novel and so I selected that.

I passed a clergyman leaving with a pile of books. The pile went up to his chin. Later I saw him again, walking down the aisles. I even went to the religious section for a moment, but couldn't understand which book to buy.

The woman who looked like me remained a stranger, as I left the city the next day. I retained an interest in secondary authors, the ones with the same last name as the people I was looking for, and bought, in one bookstore, perhaps I was in

St. Louis then, a pretty book called *Two Views* by a German named Uwe Johnson.

• • •

In St. Louis I sat outside a Laundromat while my clothes washed. A man approached. He was looking for his phone and needed me to call a friend. I called and said that I was with Robert and that he wanted to know what his phone number was. The woman on the other line asked if I was a friend of Robert's and if he was okay. Yes, he's okay, I said, I'm here with him at the Laundromat. She started to ask more. I was worried she would ask to speak to him. I didn't want to give him my phone, so I said thank you, and hung up, and handed him the number I had written down. Thank you, he said. After that I walked to an apartment where I was staying with people I didn't know. The windows were closed and while outside it had been sunny, inside it was cold and quiet. I curled on the bed and called my lover. We spoke for some time. I think mostly I talked about my fears.

The most peaceful moment of my trip happened in that city. I was on the train to East St. Louis. It was across the river and its own city; there was no reason to be there unless you belonged there. The train went across the bridge from Missouri to Illinois. It was sunny out, only a few people on the train. Only a few people ever seemed to be on the buses or trains of those cities. Two men, one sitting in front of the other, began to sing. They sang so their voices alternated; you heard one and then the other. The moment had happened by accident. They had begun a conversation, one learned the other could sing, and so they had started up. They stopped as easily as they had begun, trailing off, one saying to the other, You are good, you ever sing at your church? No, the other one said.

When I got off the train, I went into a thrift store and bought a dress and a blouse. They came to two-sixty. Then I went around back to a half-open door that went into the soup kitchen. The few people in the room stared at me. Their eyes were harder than they had been in other places. I stood in line but the food looked bad, so I only asked for a cup to get some water. Later, when I kept going to cities—Louisville, Cincinnati, Columbus, Pittsburgh—but didn't go to the soup kitchens anymore, it was East St. Louis that I thought of. I thought of St. Louis and East St. Louis, and of that thin, light-filled train that took you from one side of the river to the other.

I stayed in Memphis for a while. I didn't go to the kitchens, but I still walked around. I gave a dollar to a man on a bicycle. He was asking for money for food. He said the last man he asked gave him a cigarette, telling him it would dull his hunger. The next day he bicycled past me and tried again. I gave you money yesterday, I said.

I stayed in a hostel next to a church. For the first two nights I was in a dorm room, but I switched to a private after that. To get to the private you had to pass through a dorm. The first night the dorm was empty, but the next night a man arrived. He picked the bed closest to my door, and I could hear him turning over in the night. Rooms like that—rooms that were tucked inside other rooms, which were then part of a larger building—felt like holding, like being held by something that you couldn't see. That time in Memphis was the loneliest part of my trip, though I didn't know it then. I felt happy. I walked to the vegetarian café where the beer was two dollars after six. I read Graham Greene. On Sunday I even went to church, knowing that it could be an answer to the loneliness, but that you had to believe in order for that to be the case.

FOUR HILLS

He had the sort of face that made me check for a ring, and this wasn't easy, as I was always getting things mixed up, and which ring went on which finger, and I would stare so long at a man's hand that I was sure he'd noticed. I only checked maybe once a year, and it was only a particular kind of guy, the kind of guy who was a few years older and already had the gentleness of living with a woman, maybe had raised a child with her, and it was that gentleness, that love already existing for others, that drew me, so I knew right away that you had to look for a ring.

He had a ring, and so I told myself, There, now you know, and I felt the calm settling of disappointment as it joined the tide of all the other disappointments, the soft, great ocean of disappointment that comes from living among millions of others who also want things, sometimes the things that you want.

His face had aged into a worn beauty. He was sad; you could

just tell. He looked intently at you at first and then afterward didn't look. He had a soft voice. I had to sit close to hear him. He owned the restaurant that I applied to and was surprised to have gotten a callback for. It had been years since I waitressed, but my letter—I noticed when I reread it—was simple and direct. After meeting him I knew that he would have wanted a letter to be like that. And I was direct in person and still had the sort of appearance that drew some people. Life hadn't been quite what I wanted. I didn't have the things I would say I wanted most. I was quick and sad and you knew looking at me that nothing had gone quite right. I don't know. What do we know of ourselves? Some people noticed me in a room. Some noticed, but some didn't. I don't believe any, though, held their breath while looking at my finger. I didn't hold that sort of promise for someone: a new life briefly opening and then just as quickly closing. He was like that for me. I fell in love with his life and his restaurant—the light dimmers, the menu, the basket of aprons, the shallow soup bowls, the way the candles burned my fingers when I cleaned them, and his farm, and probably his wife and little girl, and the chef I would end up with when I couldn't be with him, and everything, everything he had, for one night, my first training shift at the restaurant.

In the city you had to work several shifts before a restaurant hired you, and I had been offered another job that I was afraid of losing. I wrote an e-mail to him, hoping he would understand. I wrote that I had to take the sure job, the one that I would lose if I waited for my second shift at his restaurant, and that I was sorry, as I liked meeting him, and liked his restaurant so much. Life never quite works out the way you want, I wrote, and I've never known what to make of it. He wrote back saying never mind about the second training shift, that if I wanted to work at his restaurant, that would be fine.

An East River Ferry terminal was near the restaurant. The ferry skirted down Brooklyn, landing in Manhattan. I used to take the ferry the other way, take it to northern Brooklyn and be let off among warehouses and duplexes painted red and blue that looked as if they were in a fishing city, some Eastern European city I'd never been to. I'd walk to a Polish café, where I'd get a square of plum cake and find a ledge or the edge of a planter where I'd sit and eat, then walk and look at the buildings. I walked wishing I lived there, near or in one of the red and blue buildings. I would narrow the city down to the river and the ferry and the circle of life around them, with little more than a café and post office and bakery and grocery store and small park to make up my world.

The ferry was never crowded. While New York was overrun with people, the ferry made me feel I was in a city that people had forgotten, where there was enough time for the man who tied up the boat to wish me a good day—every time, always a good day. Subways were so crowded I had to push through, but on the ferry I sat at a table and watched out the window, trying to decide which way the city stretched.

In the city it was a treeless fall. Even where there were trees, the colors didn't change beyond a leaden yellow. Leaves grew wet and faded and fell and were raked by the weekend crews that cleaned up after summer cookouts. It was as if the city was frozen and time was passing somewhere else. I took the train to New England to find that the trees had already lost their colors and the fields were full of pumpkins. I couldn't tell if it would have been better to stay in the city and avoid the sadness and confusion of seeing time sped up like that.

It had been a while without love, but I didn't miss it the way I used to. My last lover rarely held me, and yet that hadn't seemed sad. It was enough what we did—enough to go to the deli with the racks of doughnuts in the window and to go to parties and through undertones communicate the time we wanted to leave together. Enough time had passed that the loss of my marriage wasn't so raw anymore. On Sunday mornings, I read the Vows section of the *Times* carefully, not the simple articles of young people getting married, but about the longer, more tangled relationships, those that had been close to breaking apart. The lesson being not that love conquered all or that love was eternal, but that there was no lesson much beyond luck, timing what life gives you or doesn't.

The restaurant got its name from the owner's farm, Four Hills. The farm was north of the city, in the Hudson Valley. One day in October, I learned why it was called Four Hills. I went up with a line cook at the restaurant. It was a Wednesday, and we were both off during the day, so we drove to the farm to pick up produce. We stopped at a café that he liked and had biscuits and eggs and bacon and coffee. Grant was a quiet man. I had only noticed him when he had, on a busy night, brought my food out to tables. He was large and uncomfortable outside the kitchen, and the plates of food looked small in his hands, too small and inconsequential to be something he worked at every night.

After we ate, we drove toward the hills. The farm was nestled at the base of them, and the trees were lit in red and orange. I found I didn't want to look at them too closely.

At the farm, Grant worked like he did in the kitchen, with quick focus. Afterward, I helped carry tubs of produce and eggs to the car. Then we drove to a wine bar he knew outside of town, near the river. When he had suggested it, I had looked at my boots covered in mud, and at my jeans and jean jacket. It's fine, he had said, we're in the country.

Riding in the car, I was dazed by the trees. I told him a story of how one day, months earlier, I had taken the train to Fort Tryon Park and spent the time in the park talking about the trees. The friend I had gone with had stayed quiet. But isn't it amazing? I had said, all these trees? She had just been out of the city, she said, the week before, so maybe she was used to trees. But I hadn't been out of the city, and they seemed spectacular to me, how small and lovely you felt walking under them.

At the wine bar, we ordered at the counter and took our glasses to a deck out back. It was high up and overlooked the river. I talked about the trip I had gone on, talking about the soup kitchens and the cities, and then about being back, about the truck horns on the BQE. He was interested in food sustainability and talked for some time before stopping. I sound ridiculous, he said. I forget there are people starving in this world. He went inside and came back with a plate of toasted bread with chutney.

After, we drove back to the city. The trees had been too much, anyway. One wants trees, but not that many after so long without. We parked and carried the produce in. The owner was at a back table on his computer, drinking a glass of wine. A lot of greens, Grant told him. I went into the bathroom to change for work while Grant went to the kitchen.

Someone famous came in that night. I forget who. The food

was really beautiful, everything that we gave to this famous person. It was a good night. Enough tables for everyone to move efficiently, but not so many that the food had to be prepared too quickly. There was a hush, too, from the trip, and I moved as if still under that canopy.

The horns were incredible back then. They were the deep, sonorous creatures of the city, beckoning as if from a dream. A BQE on-ramp was close by, and drivers used my street as the access, backing up the length of it. The cars—with the twerpy horns and the rap on the radio—were annoying but forgettable, slapped away like so many pesky flies in the fall when all the flies are trying to get indoors, trying to keep alive. The trucks were different. They were the conversation the city was having with me back then, the rumbling, infernal progress of need across a landscape, of making movement heard and felt, making progress heard and felt. It created a tremor. Reminded me of how small I was. I slept and woke to those horns. Sometimes one low, steady, constant bellow would last improbably long—ten, fifteen seconds of need. The horns echoing to each other, calling to each other. I slept and woke to that.

The first night Grant stayed over, we lay in bed listening to the trucks. Like they are all lost and finding their mates, I said. It was a horrible sound, but better if you thought of it that way. The light from streetlights came in and we moved our hands through it. All the trucks trying to find each other in the night. He told me that the restaurant wasn't doing well, that it was losing the owner money and they were trying to stay afloat. Which you know, he said. Of course. Because you aren't making money either. When you're poor, I said, sometimes it becomes easier to make even less money. We weren't trying to fall asleep. We'd had sex while the light was going down and hadn't yet turned on the lights. We were getting hungry but still hadn't moved, putting off the discomfort the nudity was going to bring us. I had some money, some years ago, after the divorce, I said, some money from my ex-husband, but that's gone now.

He said he didn't want to work in kitchens anymore. He wanted to spend the winter in the farm cottage. He had planned to go to Spain, had started in kitchens to save money, but had stayed instead. It hadn't been the plan, but he was still young, and now wanted to spend a year on the farm. He said that kitchen only had a dorm fridge and a hot plate. That's what I want, he said. That's all I want. He was a strong man. You could imagine it for him. And you? he said. What foolish things do you hope for?

Something very similar, I said, not wanting to tell him otherwise, that hopes softened in time, and now mostly I thought about things I'd miss when they were gone—the smell of him, the way he moved, the street that I lived on.

In the kitchen he laid out what I had in the fridge—which wasn't much—and made a dinner of omelets and fried potatoes. After, we went out for the cheap manhattans they made at the corner bar, which weren't good, but were strong and large, and then we went back to my apartment and fell asleep, as the trucks had at last quieted, and I had drawn the curtain to darken the room.

TRAVELERS

The church was still there, not changed at all, still with the Pilgrim Travel Hostel on the upper floor and the playground behind. Our apartments—the Church Apartments—were gone, having been razed for parking. Back then, when we lived there, we could always tell the travelers. For some reason they always struggled with the lock. We would stand by our window and watch them try to get into the church. You could see, not alarm, but the warding off of alarm. They would step back and look around as if expecting someone. Richard used to bike to his job at the college. We bought the bike from one of the travelers. We kept it against the living room wall. We didn't have any money and were afraid of someone stealing it. I would be working in the living room and he would open the door and roll the bike in then sit on the sofa with his helmet still on. We didn't have very much furniture—just the couch, a coffee table. We wanted to be ready to move, I think. The apartment building was attached to the church and I found a door that went inside it. I spent time, at night, when I couldn't sleep, walking the church hallways. Richard always fell asleep right away.

The church ran a day care. During nap time, the children slept on rolled-out mats, without any pillows or blankets. They slept in rows just like that, and made crafts from colored pom-poms—making rainbows that hung from string. I liked the day care: the colored pom-poms, the snacks in Dixie cups, the day they decorated their bikes in the parking lot.

On Sundays I went to church and Richard stayed in bed, neither of us believers, but I was moved by the neighborliness of the event. The deacon had long flowing hair and flowing robes. I was afraid of her equanimity and cheerfulness, but the pastor—a thin, thinning-haired woman with hurt eyes—it was natural to like her for the stinginess of her gifts. It was the deacon who always read stories during the children's service, which was the second one of the day, the one that I went to. The pastor sat behind the altar watching as if she had been ordered to stay away.

Back then a child—a little girl named Ruth Simmons—was taken from the Pilgrim day care. After class, she had gone out in the hall with the other children and gone up to an adult. They left together, and though the teacher hadn't recognized the adult, Ruth was so natural that the teacher had thought nothing of it. I don't remember this time well, except for the pastor, not in robes anymore, but in a linen skirt and blouse in the parking lot, facing the sky as if looking for God. I would say I didn't believe in God back then, but when I thought of God I thought of the force the woman was communicating with. As if God was everything that wasn't her. To her we must be God, I thought, though I wasn't sure what I meant. Mostly back then I thought of how I wasn't good enough at any one thing. I had by then loved so much that hadn't loved me back. How was so much inequality possible? Who was loved more than it loved back? Perhaps only children. Perhaps that's why the death of a parent is so painful.

I knew little about this lost child. I kept meaning to look her up online, to see whether she was found and how. If she had been abused, left again to face an incomprehensible world. Or if some lunatic had simply tried to adopt her in the most direct way. I've always felt that parents, too, take children from some other place. I don't remember the parents from this time. The police were around. They knocked on our door. Richard told them about the place and about ourselves. That we had lived in the apartment for eight months and that he worked at the college. We hadn't seen anything, had always been happy there, though it was true, people came in and out because of the hostel, but he had never seen a bad sort. Who knows what he told the police; he had a sensible voice. Early on he thought he might be in radio. They looked about our bushes. Then knocked on the neighbor's door. You could hear the muffled voice of authority and gentle response. Not the parents, or reporters, or a change in the events of the church—the only thing I remembered was the change in the pastor. In the habit she developed of coming out the back door, the one for the hostel, and staring toward the apartments, her hair blowing.

For years after my divorce I saw a therapist who tried, carefully and slowly, to get me to talk about my father. Because we worked together for so many years, and because those times were spent traveling back—as if in a tube, a dimly felt groping for something remembered—to my childhood, I became girl-like in her presence. I became frightened when I found I had no firsthand memories. All my memories were remembered memories. In this way, I disliked talking about them. There was never a way to be certain what had happened. My father took me out on the beach. Or we were walking along the shoreline; the tide must have been out because the sand was vast, shimmering. Other people were also on the shoreline and they were far away. My father found a horseshoe crab and flipped it with a stick to show me there was nothing inside of it, but this might have been another time. But he was trying to teach me nature in a meticulous way. This probably happened. But the story I was telling was not the story itself. It was a story I knew because I had told it several times, as a description of my father, a description of his thoroughness.

There was grief, of course, in all of it. What was the point in those years spent with that woman? To access the grief, to claim it as my own and be able to move on with it? But I didn't want to do it. I turned away from the exercises in memory after a time. I simply loved her. She was diminutive. She hardly filled her chair. When she died of a brain hemorrhage I ended up calling a crisis hotline. It was weeks after the funeral. It was the first time I had ever done that. I called not because life had become unendurable, but because I wanted to know what to do in case it became unendurable. They told me I could call the hotline any time, and, if it became necessary, that they had a list of places where I could go. After that was three days spent at the Bellevue inpatient clinic with a doctor named Kurt, and then an outpatient psychiatrist I visited every month for my prescription whom I did not care for; she always got my appointments mixed up and made me wait in the hall and then filled out incorrect times on my form to make my wait appear shorter. There was a park, though, some blocks from the hospital and a Thai place that had a lunch special and the most efficient service I had ever come across.

When the girl Ruth vanished one day—never to return again—I felt it had something to do with the travelers. Not that Ruth had been taken by the travelers—as the police had carefully questioned the hostel workers and those who had come and stayed—but that Ruth was one of the travelers, that she had never been with us to stay. I walked the hallways at night and thought of why I traveled, of the feeling of suspension, of impending arrival. I understood the truth, that something terrible had taken place. I shouldn't romanticize child abductions, though what dizzying confusion it is, with those AMBER alerts texted to you at three in the morning. A child taken in a copper-colored sedan in an area of the city so far away as to be a distant land. You picture the car racing along with a child, not to anywhere horrible or real, but as if to the moon. And you stand at your window in wonderment at this luminous world. I felt the loss of the child—perhaps as a representation, of the little girl my father had left, of the little girl I had never been able to become, or of the little girl I wanted to have. These are the ways we might have talked in therapy, and I had participated willingly, hoping that it might help in some way, but mostly because I liked to talk with that gentle woman.

There were questions: Why would evil happen to children? How do we understand it and continue believing? Is there a way we can understand it? I asked the pastor these questions. I didn't know how to tell her about the travelers. I found, in the way I would find with my therapist years later—as you often find with someone you love—a common world that felt manageable. I wanted to but didn't ask: Do we get to go home? Why did it seem more likely for children, as if they were closer to the beginning when it came time to return? Maybe we had gone too far.

She didn't garden and I rarely saw her except when she was in front of the congregation on Sundays. She was never memorably eloquent. How does one get to be known as good at that job? What sense of herself or her profession did she have? I used to wonder about this. She told stories during her sermon; in one, she was in a grocery store, in the fruit aisle, faced with so many inexplicable choices. She must have tied this into faith, though I forget the moves she made. Richard disliked the church and found her interminable. I was riveted, but didn't say it. She hates being in front of people, I thought. I also couldn't understand being a true believer. It seemed the most fantastical thing, to be so full of belief in the mystical that you would go up front to teach others. Her face, the pinch of it, and her weary eyes made her seem too tired to actually be a believer.

Her office was on the second floor of the building. She was, on the day I first went up, tucked into her desk. She looked up when I came to the door. I introduced myself. Yes, I've seen you on Sundays, she said. You live in back. With my husband, I said. Yes, and your little girl, she said. No, I said quickly. We don't have a child. We would like to, but it will be some time . . . I paused and she didn't speak, though it had been her mistake. She was waiting for me to explain myself. Perhaps those of faith are used to being told—if they sit still and wait—are used to being told everything. I don't have a girl, you see, I said. Though I would like one. We're young still, I said. Too young to take in a child, I thought, imagining them as souls in a hall, waiting for someone to open the door so they could pass through, and that parents were nothing more than that, not the thing itself, not the moment of their creation. I felt that the girl had returned to the hallway to wait again.

The pastor grew up in a town in New Hampshire. Ellsworth, she said, then asked if I knew it. She took out a large green book. I waited for a theology lesson but in fact she was opening an atlas. She pointed to a dot in the middle of New Hampshire. Her mother had died and her father was an alcoholic, she said. The town had one church in the middle of a field. She never went as her father wasn't religious. It held her more, she said, than had he had religion and she had gone every week. She hadn't returned to Ellsworth in twenty years, she said, and still had never gone to the church. Though she called our time together her visiting hours and made clear it was part of her work as pastor—to attend to the spiritual needs of the community—she mostly talked about herself and her beliefs, and not in the sense that she was teaching me, but because she seemed to enjoy talking out loud. Perhaps she hadn't been given such free range in a long time.

I could see the New England in her. You could see her in a turtleneck with her face whitened with the cold. She had asked me about my childhood, and I talked about my parents. My mother was strict, I said. It was a stern upbringing, a New England upbringing. And she said, Yes, as was mine. She said her childhood would have been lonely if not for her faith, which she had from a young age. I asked her what faith felt like, what it felt like in your body, whether it had a physical sensation such as longing had. I wouldn't know, she said.

Once I felt the desire to have a baby it took me a year to realize what it was; something clinched me in a tight place in my chest and pulled me, but I didn't know what the pulling was. It wasn't what I would have guessed. That you feel the urge to have a baby and a worry that you won't be able to have a baby. Instead it feels like you'll expire; there's a sense of time running out. An urgency as if you'll die soon. I hadn't imagined that about the desire, how physical it would be. She leaned back in her chair, as if to consider, and said, I haven't felt those things. I don't know.

I was traveling once—where was I?—I was in Columbus, I think, and I came upon a historical street sign. One of those that describe a landmark. This one said Strangers Church and explained that there had been several churches that served the area hotels. I remembered it because, well, weren't they all strangers' churches? Hers had been. She was not fit for the work. The congregation didn't warm to her. She left a year or two after we left. She had a poor memory and poor facial recognition in a job where you needed both. When I had once asked her, Why did you think I had a little girl that one time? she had said that with such a changing parish, it's hard to remember most people. She usually didn't do what she had done that day—give her lack of memory away—but she had forgotten herself for a moment. It was a good guess, so many children in the congregation. You know, she said, often parents come because they want their children to grow up around faith, not because they have faith themselves. Which is not the same, she said. Not the same at all.

On the second service of the day, the deacon read to the children. The children came up and she would motion for them to sit around her. Then she would read a story that, in my memory, always involved lambs and the goodness of Jesus. She was jolly and happy and made the children comfortable. Where was the pastor during this time? Sitting back, watching.

I tried my best with my therapist to remember what had taken place in the Church Apartments. Our living room that didn't have any furniture. The services I went to sometimes, mostly alone, because neither of us had religion but I liked the quiet hall and the pews that were engraved with names of deceased relatives. My nocturnal habits. The long hallways. The room with the children, and the parents standing outside, waiting to take the children away. What did Richard do during this time? she asked, pointing out that when I told stories, he wasn't there. You must have been lonely, she said. But he was at work; the silence and hard work no doubt helped him as the hallways helped me. We are all lost. Why blame him? It was silly to remember the stories of us not getting along. The melodrama of any couple breaking apart. My feelings for the man who stayed for a month in the neighboring apartment who made jewelry. He lay earrings on the bedspread and let me pick a pair. Feathers I picked and even wore. Mistaking the relief from loneliness that meeting another fragile soul can bring about, mistaking that for love, but who's to say it wasn't love, or what I felt for Richard, that it was love. Who's to say.

Before my husband and I left Portland, I went to say good-bye to the pastor. She was tired that day and struggling to write the sermon. She said that sometimes it came and she could feel the words inside her. But lately, she said, it had become harder for her. It felt as if words were not inside her. I wondered if that meant the faith was also not there, but didn't ask. She had told me she never doubted her faith, that there could be no crisis of faith, that it would feel like not being alive. She sometimes thought that she wasn't a good pastor. That the faith in her was a private thing and sometimes she didn't want to talk about it, though sometimes she did.

When I learned that she had left the church, left the faith, and gone back to New Hampshire, I imagined her at the grocery store. Examining the range of fruit in confusion—the watermelon, so alien to the climate, holding it and then having no one to tell about it later. To sit at home at her table by the window. Perhaps the most important thing is to have someone to tell things to. But no, she had faith, she would have felt herself in conversation all the time. Sometimes I thought that maybe I had faith and simply didn't identify that when I talked in my mind—and I talked all the time—that I hadn't identified who I was talking to, not allowed myself to feel the presence there. I had considered this one day when I was walking in the new city I had moved to. In this city there was an elevated train that I was always catching sight of in the distance. It was, sometimes, when the light was right, a magical place. The elevated train, the distant Amtrak tracks, all the children, who, in my imagination, were also in elevated places, as if there were elevated playgrounds, too. I walked and thought, Maybe I should have a child. Or maybe all this, this is always a response, only I'm not hearing it properly.

BOSTON

There is one last story that I have been trying to tell: what happened to the man who ran away from his kids on the island. When I told my mother the story, she said that the way it was left led her to believe he had killed himself. My mother rarely lets on that she is curious about what is around her—curious about anything abstract, not immediately a part of her day—but sometimes she would show that she knew quite well what was around her. She would reveal it as matter-of-factly as she revealed anything else, such as what was going on at her friend's or the neighbor's.

I tried to figure out the story about the man when I was lying in bed, tired from waitressing, but I drifted off and turned the television to a crime drama. In those dramas the lost person was always found or the crime solved. Occasionally a story wouldn't be solved, but only because it was part of a larger narrative that would be solved later. The curious thing, though, was that the solving, while mandatory, was the least interesting part of the show. I watched an endless number of episodes and for years cut clippings from newspapers about lost people. The real life stories—those newspaper clippings—never let me down, whether they were solved or unsolved. The details were too beautiful. Too etched in. Each person had only that one time to be lost, while the writers of the dramas wrote a new episode each week.

I left the story with the man from the island stealing a car. He drove to New Hampshire and stayed in abandoned houses. He wandered the houses and one day found a full closet and traded his coat for a warmer one. He also pocketed some old photographs. When the cold became unbearable, he drove to a shelter. Nothing after that, no more mention of him. He was simply in line for the shelter. Later a body was found in a lake with the warmer coat on and several photographs in a plastic bag. The owner of the coat and photographs was found alive. He couldn't account for the body in the lake—he didn't know anyone who was missing. Then he remembered his parents' home, left empty, and drove there with the officer, where they found a strange coat and pieced together what happened. As if finding a coat were finding a person. Maybe by saying it here, I can stop with that story. So often stories don't work.

It's quite a thing to think about, my mother said. She was visiting from the Cape. The subletter had left weeks earlier and my mother was staying in his room. He had moved out when I was away, leaving only a necklace pinned to the wall. It was a tiny room. My mother sat on the bed while I sat on the floor. She looked around and said it reminded her of when we had lived on the island. There was a place where we could pick grapes, she said. I was pregnant with you that summer, and I thought all the time about how you would be able to pick grapes.

I talked about the restaurant, my worry that it wasn't going to last the winter. That it had been my plan to save thirty thousand dollars to have a baby, but now there weren't enough customers.

Thirty thousand dollars wouldn't have paid for a baby, she said.

I know, I said.

The next morning I put cream and sugar on the table while my mother started the percolator. I told her I had dreamed that night about returning to Berlin, and she asked if I remembered Poland. All that way, she said, and you didn't leave the hotel. There's no reason to believe things will always go that way, I said.

We left the house for the Neue Galerie to meet up with a friend of hers. We looked at the work of an artist who painted the same lover over a period of twenty years. He had been married and never painted the wife. He was from Belgium, or a similar country, and to be in rooms with his large paintings was to be surrounded by the inner world of a man I didn't know. My mother spoke little over lunch, so I talked with her friend Robin. She wore a broad scarf around her shoulders. I was glad that my mother had never resorted to scarves. We talked about art and travel while my mother drank coffee and picked at her cake. Afterward, after saying good-bye to the woman and getting on the train, I was exhausted.

And the art, you liked it? my mother asked.

I felt bad for the wife, I said.

It's not easy for anyone, is it? she said. You liked Robin, though, you got along well with her?

You were quiet, I said.

I don't know why.

The art?

Sometimes I wonder if you would have been happier with someone like her.

She didn't mean it as a question. She said it to herself, looking out the window, and I didn't respond. I was thinking of the man who had spent all those years painting the lover and never once the wife.

That Saturday the man at the market had clams. There, my mother said, as she stepped forward and bought two dozen. At home, I scrubbed clams and put them on a towel, while she opened a bottle of chardonnay we had bought at the discount store. The wine tasted of pear juice. She was leaving the next morning. We sat at the table in the fading light and I tried to talk about Richard, put in mind of him, I think, by the clams, and the cold, and of having my mother there, and of having her about to go.

When I had spent the winter in Provincetown—it was when my marriage was ending and a painting friend had offered her cottage cheaply—I used this friend's license to clam every Sunday, going at first out of curiosity, and then because I loved it, and then after that, when the wind became bitter, the clams scarce, the ice on the jetty treacherous, simply because I didn't know what else to do.

Much of my money that winter went to the heating bill and food and beer at the Governor Bradford, which wasn't cheap—nothing in Provincetown was cheap, though it seemed like there were only seven of us staying for the winter, and none of us had any money. Everything should have been given away.

I didn't bring my computer, but I did bring pens and my notebook, which more than leading to creating anything, mostly helped alleviate the panic that I wasn't creating. The Stop & Shop was two miles away and I'd walk with my backpack and come home to cook lunch, and perhaps I'd write something or sketch with my friend's supplies. Afternoons I'd walk until stopping to have a drink at the Governor Bradford. There weren't happy hour specials in Provincetown, but being in New York had put me in the habit of drinking at dusk. Then at night I'd listen to the radio or read the *Times* or fiction from the library.

I didn't get along with the bartender at the Governor Bradford. She stiffened when I came in and was slow to greet me. At first she had been easy with me—probably thinking I was a tourist there for only a week—and told me stories about herself and the area. When she had learned that I researched stories she asked what they were about. I tried to think of something that would be easy to describe, and I talked about a girl who had gone missing from the pier in Portland. The bartender froze in place. She said, Several of my friends left here and walked off the pier. I thought of the pier, two dark blocks from the bar, how you could hear and feel the ocean and what it must have felt like.

I went to the Governor Bradford most nights until Richard came to visit and then my habits changed. We were happy then—during those two weeks—and switched to a bar across the street where younger locals went, and day trippers, and professionals from neighboring towns. There was a raw bar and microbrews, and it was warm and nice to sit by the window and eat oysters.

In the cottage, we fell in together as easily as if we were

still married, when we used to stay out late and sleep until noon and play records from bed. He would lie there, one hand lifting records from the floor and putting them on the player, which was also on the floor and covered with dust, so all our record players—and we went through a lot of them back then—played too slowly. In Provincetown, he lay there while I sat and smoked and watched out the window, talking to him, telling him stories about my childhood. I touched his back tentatively, unsure of what I wanted. He didn't move, either toward me or away. We might have been drinking the night before. He was not a big drinker, but there were a few nights he was hungover and slower in the morning. I wondered if I was mistaking his slowness for intimacy.

There was a window over the door, and another near the bed, covered with a gauze fabric that brought to mind cheesecloth. I smoked with my feet under me and watched out the window. Maybe it is cheesecloth, I said. He lay with his head down and eyes closed. What else do you see? he said. I told him about the seagulls, the clouds, the different shades of gray that made up the landscape there.

We went to the Old Colony the night they closed for the season. They turned off their fridges and put beer on the counter and you could buy anything for two dollars. They also turned their heat off, but space heaters blew air into the dark room. It was as if they had already closed, then opened to make fifty more dollars. He had loved that, sitting on a chair against the wall in his wool coat. That night he told me—we were sitting at the bar and he was holding a drink and he moved the bottle away from his mouth to say it—I'm going to take the bus out in the morning. Okay, I said. He got us both a shot of whiskey. Of Evan Williams. They didn't have beer and shot specials in

Provincetown like they did in New York; we had to buy everything separately.

The P & B bus for Boston left at six thirty in the morning, in the dark, from the harbor. He stayed up all night, working in the living room, while I slept for a few hours. I got up at six and went to the kitchen to make coffee. You don't need to be up now, he said. It's fine, I said, walking past him. We walked to the harbor holding coffee in travel mugs, and he had his bag over one shoulder. I wore a long coat over my pajamas. The bus was already there, idling. We drank coffee standing near the door of the bus. The harbor like that, in the dark, felt like a wild animal. You heard it and felt it—the dark abyss of it. Sometimes it felt like the wildest place on earth. He lurched onto the bus in the way he had of moving, as if breaking something that was attaching him to where he was.

My mother and I talked on the phone several times a week. Sometimes we'd start in midconversation. There's not much furniture in here, my mother said when I answered the phone one day, not long after she had visited. I'm sitting on the kitchen floor, she said.

She was, it turned out, housesitting a cottage on a lake for the winter. She knew the owner from Puritans, the store where she worked. Ever since those years of living on the ocean, she had wanted to see water when she woke up. Ocean property had grown so expensive. Even a lake she couldn't afford. You should come here for a time, she said. The previous tenants left boxes in the attic.

Going through other people's stuff?

Part of the deal is that I clean the place out, she said. He said I could keep anything I wanted.

Is there anything good?

No, not really. But you should come. There might be something of the sort that you like. Or maybe she had said, Something up your alley.

When I arrived—a week or two later, the restaurant had shut down and I wasn't working anymore—she was wearing surprisingly fashionable clothes though she wouldn't have known it, only recognizing them as clothes from years ago. She had on high-waisted jeans and a T-shirt and her hair was held back by a scarf.

Those sorts of pants are in again, I said.

With who? she asked.

In the city, people have started to wear those.

Not skinny jeans anymore?

It's transitioning.

There we go then, she said. I found them in the boxes. And I may have found a mystery for you, she said. Something you might like.

In the boxes?

Yes, something in the boxes.

She talked about the mystery after dinner. Her dinners were always tidy—baked chicken, salad in small bowls where most things, even the carrot shreds, came from bags and were slightly dried out, and then fluffy rolls, a bottle of ice-cold chardonnay that she had opened days ago. After we ate, she loaded the dishwasher, wiped and dried the table, then sat down. I asked if she minded if I taped her. You're working again, then? she said.

I'm not sure. Maybe.

When I turned the recorder on, her voice became loud and dutiful. There are some people who are natural being recorded, but my mother wasn't one of them. She said that she had found photographs of children standing in front of her house, sitting near the sliding door, standing before the lake. They were a boy and a girl—blond and happy. She thought they were childhood pictures of the teenagers next door. She had watched them before they left for the season. They were working at a camp and had its name on their hats and sweatshirts. The dad would grill, and then the children would leave for town in a jeep.

My mother said that she had waited for the family to leave for the season before swimming in the lake. Sometimes the father came on the weekend to do projects. She took the pictures to him. He—Ian—was in front of his house, putting in a new mailbox. She told him that she had found the photographs and wondered if they were his kids. He didn't hold the photographs as his hands were dirty, so she held them. Then he went inside to wash his hands. When he came back, he asked if he could keep them and she said yes, that was why she had brought them over.

She got to know him as the fall went on. She would be out raking and he would be out raking. Or they would both get the mail. Those sorts of things. They would talk about the weather, or the town, or what getting older entailed. Once he said that if he had acted peculiar that day, when she had brought over the pictures, it was only because he wasn't sure they were his kids. They looked like them, but not enough, for some reason, that he knew right away. He said, Isn't that something you should know?

One day, when we came back from shopping in town, Ian was in his yard. He had just arrived for the weekend. I hadn't met him yet. The three of us stood on the lawn; she introduced me, I shook his hand, then my mother and I went into the house, carrying groceries. I sat at the table while she made lunch. Afterward she wiped and dried the table, then laid out photographs, having kept several of them. I studied them, then asked what she supposed. I don't know, my mother said. I thought you would like them.

I thought, She must be lonely. There was hardly any furniture and trees kept light out. It had the economy she wanted. She said to me at some point—maybe when she was handwashing dishes because she only had two of everything and we had wanted to eat salad in bowls after eating soup—I'm sorry that I'm not something different. You think it wouldn't pain me to keep four bowls.

Looking at the pictures on the table, I talked about my interest in doubling—that reality could have been altered slightly, leaving traces of another. For instance, his children, at the time those pictures were taken, could have been somewhere else, but that didn't mean those weren't also his children.

I thought about it later, on my mattress on the floor. I wasn't trying to explain the pictures. I was trying to explain another world, one I had always wanted to find. One day, when we were in Provincetown, Richard and I had broken into a dune shack. I had stood inside, looking out the window at the ocean. I didn't move, even as he tried to show me things he had found. He asked if I was okay. We lived in so many houses when I was a little girl, I said. What was I feeling? Desire, maybe. To want something that you couldn't remember. It was a hard feeling to live with. After the divorce, I saw light everywhere. Some light—the light at the end of the day, the way it hit the pigeons that flew around the steeple, the way it hit the sides of buildings—that light felt like entrances to another world. Like the shack had felt when I was looking out the window. Sometimes it was better to be farther from this feeling. I felt it would split me if I let it.

In the morning, when I woke, chilled, on the floor, I didn't know where I was. I pulled the recollection from bits around me. I walked to the kitchen and from the window saw my mother talking to the man next door. She held a coffee mug and he, a rake. A leaf blew in her hair and he picked it out and she smiled. They stood still. He touched her hair again. She reached up and touched his hand. They stood holding hands, and then she turned to come inside, their grasp loosening as she pulled away.

I asked if she had eaten breakfast. Some toast, she said, but I would have a little more with you.

I was going to make a full thing, I said, at least if you have things to make French toast with.

She found a skillet and a plastic spatula that had melted some and a plastic mixing bowl, then went into her room to change, coming out in a wool skirt and turtleneck sweater. We ate French toast and clementines. How is Ian? I asked.

Fixing the drain, she said. He asked if I needed anything from Home Depot. Do we need anything? Besides mousetraps?

I drove her to work at Puritans so that I could use her car and from there drove farther out, first to a thrift store to buy items she was missing—a can opener, a strainer—then to the swap shop at the dump to look at clothing, considering an oversized coat made in Yugoslavia, and then thought, Enough of coats. I read in the town library, then went to pick up my mother, stopping inside the store to watch her. She had the habit of looking as if she was studying the women around her for how to act. She straightened a stack of sweaters while the other two employees talked by the desk.

Outside it had grown dark. We drove to a bar on Main Street with stained glass windows and plank walls. Inside felt snug and warm. We got stouts and she talked about work, of the coworker that was always complaining about her boyfriend and also about a neighbor who had been arrested for guns. Mom, I said, with Ian. Am I interrupting something by being here? Would it be better if I went?

What do you mean? she said.

I could leave tomorrow, or I'm grown now, you could just go over.

He's married.

That kind of thing. It's one of those things. It is what it is.

We could go down Cape tomorrow, she said. There's a show at PAAM of artists who painted the light in Provincetown.

You're always taking me to shows.

I always think you like them, she said.

Do you?

Sure. They're fine.

You noted, right, that I let it go?

I noted it, my mother said.

I dreamed that I had a baby—that it simply popped out; there was no terrible birth, no pain, even in the dream I was aware of the unlikeliness of what had happened—and when the baby wanted milk, I called for my mother because I didn't know how to nurse.

I didn't tell my mother about the dream. What she would have said. Maybe I loved her best because she believed the things

I said. She even took my dreams as fact. Well, she would have said, You just figure it out. It's just something that happens.

It's impossible to see your mother as a middle-aged man might see her. To see her as a girl grown older. But I still tried to imagine it. At the beginning of fall, when the mornings were growing cold and the family next door had gone away—going back to their town outside Boston, leaving only the man to weatherproof the house—my mother had taken to swimming. She had an old red suit, the material softened by age. From a distance she probably looked like a flag. She would have worn a towel until she got near the water and then dropped it to wade in. The man next door would have noticed it one morning and then taken to making coffee by the window overlooking the lake. He had an estranged marriage—he was there, after all, at the summer cottage while his wife and kids were back home—and my mother would have been easy company. She was spare, self-sufficient. And she was such a small woman; she must have looked like a girl emerging from the water. He would have started with offers—to get her groceries, to help nail a shutter—and then would have offered his dock to dive off.

What I missed most when I lost a man I loved was someone who held a record of my life from that time. It was the way we told each other things. Without them I went back to my quiet life, but with them there was a transcript of living. *Transcript,* of all words, as a way to describe love. But we all want, in some way, to be able to record our life, and for some reason lovers do that for each other. Of all things. Of all jobs for them to be given.

My mother and I drove down Cape the next day, to the study-of-light exhibit, and when she saw that it hadn't made me happy, that I hadn't found the art good, had found it a small-town exhibit, she mentioned a theater show she heard was quite good in Chatham. I said, It's okay, Mom, I'm just here to see you. Me, she said. Me of all things. We stopped at the lighthouse and kicked off our shoes and walked along the coastline, clutching our jackets and not talking because of the wind. When we got in the car she paused and said, They had been separated, but then were together over the summer with the kids, but they're separated again, which is why he's staying here.

Will he be staying for a long time? I asked.

I don't know, my mother said.

The clouds were going over the sun in the incredible way that happened there. The study of light, I pointed out, this is worth a thousand of those shows.

I'd like to think she said something like, Maybe forever, maybe it will stay like this forever, but of course she wouldn't have. She would had said something careful. Who's to say how long any of this lasts, she might have said. It's nice to have company. I'm going to enjoy it while I'm here. All lines I've said myself at one time or another, and no doubt I meant them, too, when I said them.

The last story I have about my father I have from her, so it's a story with little embellishment, even less emotion, and the kind of odd detail that seeks to compensate, as the person telling the story must linger on something after all. She said that after my father left us, she visited him a few times with me and my brother. He had gone to Boston where he got temporary jobs. She would take us there, and we would sit, and he would say, Well, you must be hungry, and she would say, No, not really, as we had eaten on the drive. She said that we were in the habit, when driving to Boston, of going to Friendly's, as we liked the clown sundaes. Once we hadn't stopped for food and she said that we would eat something if he made it, and he put mustard and American cheese on white bread and cut it into triangles. He served peach juice from Dixie cups.

Then he moved and for fifteen years she didn't hear from him, but one day he got in touch, and she drove to Boston to see him, not telling me, as she wanted to see him first. He had found work as a janitor. My mother had brought a picture of us, but later, when she got home, realized she hadn't shown him. He had changed. He had gotten older and his health had grown bad. The apartment was cold, the building vacant. The building was to be torn down and the owners were allowing him to live there in the meantime. There were several pianos. She asked if he played and he said they weren't tuned, but that when he came across one he couldn't help himself. There were boxes everywhere. He asked after me. How is Anne? She realized she still hadn't sat down, that she wasn't comfortable, and, remembering a deli she had passed, suggested they get something to eat. Or she suggested an Irish bar she had seen around the corner. But he pointed to his feet and said he didn't have shoes on. She was about to say that he could just put them on, but then stopped. She thought, Maybe he has the thing where you can't go out. She had been alive long enough to have felt that, felt the terror of the world around you, some form of that, some form of most things.

That afternoon they talked about easy matters. Friends he had, those who helped bring in the pianos and brought other things for him now that he had trouble working. And then about me. That I was away. And that when I came back we would come and visit. That I would want to see him. She said that if he wanted we could all go to a restaurant. He was mostly quiet. When I asked her, Would he have wanted to see me? She said, Of course. He just didn't know how to say it. She wrote him a letter a month later, but it got returned, so she drove to Boston, only to find the house had been boarded up. She looked in one window, but the pianos were gone. She said, After a time, I thought maybe I had the wrong house, or maybe I hadn't seen him at all.

ACKNOWLEDGMENTS

• • •

I am indebted to the teaching and support I received from the Provincetown Fine Arts Work Center, the Bennington Writing Seminars, and the University of Massachusetts–Amherst Program for Poets and Writers. Thank you to friends and family who helped with this book, including Sam Leader, Brian Booker, Allison Devers, Katherine Hill, Anu Jindal, Emily Hunt, Dan Bevacqua, the St. Botolph Club Foundation, Inpatient Press, and John Cochary. Special thanks to Brigid Hughes and Jonathan Lee, who made this book possible.

SARA MAJKA'S stories have appeared in *A Public Space, PEN America,* the *Gettysburg Review,* and *Guernica.* A former fiction fellow at the Fine Arts Work Center in Provincetown, she lives in New York City.

Cities I've Never Lived In was set in Adobe Caslon.
Book design by Rachel Holscher.
Composition by Bookmobile Design & Digital
Publisher Services, Minneapolis, Minnesota.
Manufactured by Versa Press on acid-free,
30 percent postconsumer wastepaper.